# Saving Levi

## Kaci Rose

D0870589

Five Little Roses Publishing

# Copyright

companies, events, institutions, or locales is completely coincidental.

Book Cover By: **Sweet N Spicy Designs**

Editing By: Debbe @ **On the Page, Author and PA Services**

Proofread By: Ashley @ **Geeky Girl Author Services**

# Blurb

I dated her best friend in high school. That makes her an automatic no-no. Don't go there, right?

*Wrong.*

I can't stop thinking about her.

We're friends. Best friends. She's the one I can talk to. For a guy like me, in this life, that's priceless. Especially since I just was discharged from the military with an injury that's changed my life.

She's precious to me, but I can't go there.

Right?

The only problem is, I *can't stop thinking about her.*

# Dedication

To all the men and women serving our country, past and present. To their friends and families who support them daily.

# Contents

# Get Free Books!

Do you like Military Men? Best friends brothers?
What about sweet, sexy, and addicting books?

**If you join Kaci Rose's Newsletter you get these books free!**
**https://www.kacirose.com/free-books/**
**Now on to the story!**

# Chapter 1

## Mandy

Not only do I love Oakside, but I love helping the people here. I've been here from the beginning, and helping Lexi and Noah set it all up and, watching it grow from what it was to what it is now is something I was so happy to see.

What I don't like are the late nights when we're having budget problems and trying to figure out how to expand and help even more people. I guess I should clarify when I say we're having budget problems. It's not that we don't have enough money. It's that we just got a pretty big donation, and we're not quite sure the best way to allocate it just yet.

I've spent several late nights budgeting it out only to go back to work in the morning and everyone's decided to go a different way, and I have to redo it all over again. That's still on top of lining up all the events and doing my other daytime work of setting up events and bringing in not only a steady stream of income but awareness.

As I don't have anything to go home to I don't mind, so having dinner in my office is no big deal to me. When Lexi and Noah built Oakside, they did this place up right, especially where the office is. Even though we are technically in the basement, it doesn't feel like it with as much natural light as they were able to bring in.

Sitting back in my chair, I stretch as my neck pops back into alignment. Then I turn in my leather chair and look at my bookshelves. These were the one thing that Lexi splurged on just for me, an entire wall of bookshelves. They're all in white, which makes the place even more beautiful, and while at the moment there aren't enough books to fill the shelves, I filled it up with pictures of my family and friends.

There are also a lot of pictures of different events that I've hosted here as well, like the Halloween haunted house we did a few months ago, and the huge Christmas celebration, Oakside's first Christmas event.

I'm so lost in thought, I don't notice anyone else is down here.

"Mandy?" I hear a voice call my name from the door.

I glance quickly at the door, realizing it's a patient. If they needed anything they should have gotten it from their nurse upstairs. This man is in a wheelchair, so that means he took the elevator and knew that he was coming down here where we don't allow patients, especially this time of night. Turning back to my computer, I don't pay attention to who it is.

"Patients aren't allowed down here," I say.

It's a general rule of thumb. Even though their offices are down here, Lexi and Noah are always upstairs. There are a few other offices down here, like the kitchen, an employee lounge, and a locker room with a changing area. But in general, it's all staff and we don't allow patients down here.

"I know, but I was trying to sneak down for a midnight snack," he chuckles.

I glance up from the computer to tell him to go back upstairs and ask his nurse for a midnight snack. It's not that we don't want them to eat or allow them to; it's that for insurance purposes we don't let patients down here in the kitchen where they could hurt themselves. Especially patients who might be unsteady due to their injuries.

When I finally look at his face, I realize that I know him and not just because he's a patient here.

"Levi?" I ask.

There is no way that this is the same Levi that I went to school with. The one that my best friend dated and went to prom with only to break up because he was going into the military, and she was going away to college. We also shared a lot of the same friends growing up because we're from a small town.

"Yeah, I was starting to think you didn't recognize me." He chuckles and wheels himself into my office. "Why are you here so late?"

"Budgets. We keep changing them and it takes work to balance it on top of everything else I do. It's quietest after dinner and the best time to work with numbers," I shrug.

"You work here?" he asks.

"Yeah. I'm the charity coordinator, but being we are still pretty small, I take on a few other jobs as needed too."

Those jobs include budgeting, accounting, event planning, or whatever else Lexi and Noah need me to do.

Looking him over, I can see he's lost part of his leg from just below the knee down. I'm guessing that's why he's here, to learn to walk again with a prosthetic.

"After you and Rebecca broke up, I had heard you joined the military, but I hadn't heard anything about you since."

"Yeah, I was set to go to college after graduation, but I realized that wasn't the life I wanted. So, I joined up and was off to boot camp just over a week later, so very few people knew."

"What branch?" I ask.

"Army. Got this while on patrol one day and now here I am." He says, tapping his knee where he lost part of his leg.

I start to hear people stirring around downstairs, but still wanting to talk to Levi, I make a quick decision.

"Why don't you come in, close the door and keep me company?"

With a smile on his face, he comes in, closing the door with ease. He seems to have mastered being in the wheelchair, which means he's been here longer than just a few days. I normally know all the patients, but being so busy I haven't been upstairs mingling as much as I should.

"How long have you been here?" I ask, trying to remember the last time I was even upstairs.

"They transferred me here just a few days before Christmas."

"That was over two months ago," I say more to myself than to him.

"Yeah, I'm surprised I haven't seen you before."

"Normally I try to get upstairs and mingle and talk to patients at least once a day. But closing out the year, having to file all of our company paperwork, and with this budget, I just lost track of time. I hadn't realized it's been that long since I've been upstairs."

Levi offers me a smile and shrugs it off.

"Are you still friends with Rebecca?" he asks.

Not quite sure how to respond, since Rebecca is now married and they are expecting their first kid. If he's hoping to reconnect, I want to let him down lightly. But just the fact that he's asking about Rebecca makes my gut churn, and I'm not quite sure why.

"Yeah, we lost contact while in college since we went to different places, but we reconnected recently on Facebook. I found out she lives only about an hour away, so we've met up several times. Though she's married now with their first kid on the way, and she's really happy." I say, watching his reaction.

Either he's very good at covering his emotions or he really wasn't all that interested in her and was just trying to make small talk because I don't see an ounce of sadness or regret on his face. Honestly, he smiles more than I thought he would.

"I'm glad she's happy. I always felt bad about how we ended things because she wasn't overly thrilled with me going into the military and never wanted to be a military girlfriend. Can't blame her as I don't think she would have handled this whole thing very well if she was still my girl."

He's not wrong. Rebecca wasn't the type of person that did well in stressful situations, and she fainted at the sight of blood. She refused to step foot in a hospital, and she hated flying. So, if they were still together, getting the phone call that Levi was hurt would have gone pretty badly.

Not sure what to say and wanting to change the subject I pull out a Tupperware container of cookies that I have in my drawer for a snack. The sugar keeps me going when I don't want to drink coffee but need a little bit of a boost to get me through the rest of the night. Taking the top off, I hold it out to him.

"Would you like a cookie? Though I can't allow you to go into the kitchen, I can offer you these. I made them myself."

He gives me another grin and wheels himself forward, taking a cookie. I notice he's smiling a lot in a place like this where everyone is working through their own injuries. One thing you don't see is a lot of smiles. Mostly, you have a lot of angry people with a lot of cussing and even some crying, but smiles are few and far between.

We sit there for a few hours and chat, catching up on old friends that we used to hang out with. He talked about old times in school.

"Did you ever keep up with your prom date?" Levi asks as he finishes off the last cookie.

"Who, Jeremy? No, prom was our first date, and he thought he was going to get lucky because it was prom. I ended up punching him in the face before the night was over and going home alone."

That has Levi laughing uproariously.

"If I have known, he would have had more than just a punch in the face. Heck, any of our friends that we hung out with would gladly have had your back. He would have ended up with a few broken bones."

"I know. Though I had told Rebecca and made her swear not to tell anybody for that reason."

I fight off a yawn and realize it is much later than I realized.

"Well, I need to get home and you need to get back to your room." I give him a pointed stare.

"I'm on my way." He backs out of the room and heads back upstairs as I gather up my stuff.

"Hey, Levi?" I say before he leaves. He stops and looks back over his shoulder.

"Yeah?"

"If you're interested, I'll have more cookies tomorrow."

Another huge smile crosses Levi's face.

"I'll be here."

He goes up to his room while I gather my stuff, heading out to my car to go home. On the way, all I can think about is how happy he was and how he seems almost too happy. While he seems completely okay with what's happened to him, I know what other patients have gone through and I have to wonder if it's an act.

If it is, then it's going to be that much longer before he heals, not just physically, but mentally. He might be completely okay with losing his leg and having to learn to walk again on a prosthetic, but that doesn't mean that his mind is all right with what happened and how it happened. Both have to be healed before they release him and if he's just covering up what's going on mentally with a bunch of smiles, it's going to be that much longer that he's here.

Getting home, I walk into my empty two-bedroom cottage. It's my first home and the first place I was able to buy on my own. I got it at such a great price because it needed work done. Of course, Lexi volunteered her brother and her dad to help with the renovations on the house and they have been a godsend. Like when a pipe burst in the bathroom at two o'clock a.m., they didn't hesitate to send someone out to help fix it so that I could take a shower in the morning.

As I'm lying in bed, I'm still thinking about Levi. I remind myself to make a note to talk to Lexi. At the very least, she should be made aware that we know each other. The fact that we're acquainted could either help or hinder his rehabilitation. We have seen it go both ways.

The thought of maybe calling Rebecca and telling her that Levi is at Oakside also runs through my mind. But Levi may not want to see her, and I know that if she knows he's here she would rush in to make sure he's okay. So, I decide to leave that out of the topics the next time that we talk.

Over the next week, Levi joins me downstairs for some cookies as well as keeping me company when I stay late. After a while, it becomes a little routine and one that I'm looking forward to.

Too bad I couldn't keep it to just that and had to push the envelope.

# Chapter 2

## Mandy

Every night we have cookies and we'll sit and talk in between me getting some work done. We've spent the time just catching up on what everyone's doing, his time in the military, my time away at school, and even how I ended up here at Oakside and some of the events that I've helped with before he came.

We have been talking a bit about Lexi and Noah and their story. He was also curious about Easton and Paisley since Easton was a patient here and he knew Paisley growing up. I told him how their romance was fun to watch evolve. Now that they're married, those two are pretty much inseparable.

Easton is in charge of security here at Oakside and Paisley still works with patients who could benefit from therapy dogs. The two of them are always a hit when they're here because the patients love both of their dogs.

Paisley trained Easton's dog, Allie, who is always at Easton's side. Paisley also trained her own dog, Molly. While Molly isn't Paisley's service dog, she's trained to help the soldiers, and Paisley takes her into the hospital and does volunteer work with her.

It's almost lunchtime and I'm sitting in my office, hesitating. Though I know I need to go upstairs and mingle, it's hard to make myself do it. Today I made a lunch for Levi. He had mentioned that it had been a while since he had a home-cooked meal. Something inside me wanted to cook for him to make sure he didn't feel alone here.

When I told Lexi about me knowing Levi, she was really excited. I guess he hasn't had any visitors, and they were a little worried. I've been wanting to ask Levi about his parents, but keep hesitating because anytime the subject gets around to his parents, he changes the subject. I have a feeling that bringing it up wouldn't be welcome nor anything he wants to talk about.

Finally getting up the courage, I take my food container from my mini-fridge and make my way upstairs. It's one thing for Levi to join me downstairs for cookies, but I haven't been upstairs to his room yet so I'm not sure how he'll take it.

As usual, Lexi is at the front desk. She sees me and gives me a huge smile.

"And she emerges from her cave. It's been a while since we've seen you on this side," Lexi laughs.

"I know, I know. If you guys would stop messing with the budget and changing where you want to spend the money, I would actually be able to step out of my office every once in a while." Even though she knows I'm just playing around, at the same time, it's the truth.

"So now would it be a good time to tell you that we've decided to go in a new direction?"

Lexi's voice is so serious I freeze. I'll work out any budget they want, but if they really did change their minds again, the chances that I would strangle her right now are pretty high. I take a deep breath, trying to decide exactly what to say.

"I'm just kidding with you. I promise," Lexi says with a big smile lighting up her face.

I sag in relief.

"You can't do that to me! I'm not getting enough sleep." I hold up the food container. "I decided to bring Levi some food and maybe try to talk to him a little bit. What room is he in?"

Since Lexi is always involved in everything that goes on here, as is Noah, she doesn't even have to look up Levi's room number. She just rattles it off the top of her head. It's on the ground floor because he's in a wheelchair so I go down the hallway off the lobby.

On this side of the building, the residents staying on the ground floor have their own private courtyard that isn't open to guests. As you walk down the hallway, one side is all glass windows overlooking the courtyard. Making sure Levi isn't out there, I glance out before heading on to his room.

When I find him in his room looking out his window, I clear my throat to get his attention. He turns to look at me but doesn't offer me a smile or even ask what I'm doing there.

"You mentioned the other day that you couldn't remember the last time you had a home-cooked meal. So, I brought you some of my meatloaf for lunch. Would you like me to warm it up for you?"

He just nods, so I turn, leaving the room and go to a small utility room that has a microwave, mini-fridge, and a few other things that the nurses might need. After warming up the food up and putting it on one of the plates, I grab a roll of silverware and go back to his room.

He's still in the same spot, but he's turned in facing the doorway. So I slowly step into his room and place the food on the coffee table near him. He just watches every move that I make but doesn't say a word. Over the past week, he's let his beard grow just a little bit. Several times I thought that it looks sexy on him and then I've had to correct myself. We're just friends.

"Everything all right?" I ask as he slowly nods his head.

"Thank you for the lunch, but if you don't mind, I'd like to eat alone. Can you close the door on your way out?"

I nod, doing as he asks, and close the door on my way out. Even though I'm not quite sure what they were, I think that those were the first real emotions that I've seen from him. Then I have to wonder if he's like this all day and just happy-go-lucky when he comes to visit me at night or if he's just having a bad day.

Deciding to stop and ask Lexi about it before going back to my office, I walk up to the reception desk where she's sitting, and once again she offers me one of her huge smiles. Lexi is one of those people that love helping other people. It's why she started Oakside.

"Did he like the food?"

"I don't know. He wanted to eat alone, and it doesn't seem like he's having a good day."

"I noticed that too," Lexi says. "He seems off but I'm not sure why. Even though I've asked, he won't talk, so I'm not pushing it. His doctors have been notified, so it's best to let them handle it."

"Well, I'm going to go eat at my desk and get some work done. I'll come back up and get his plate and check on him after a while. I have some cookies that might cheer him up."

I'm only sitting at my desk for a minute before my phone rings. Glancing at the caller ID, I see that it's Rebecca, and almost don't pick up. Though it's not her fault that I feel weird talking to her now, but I still don't think I should tell her that Levi is here or that I've recently run into him.

"Hey Rebecca, how are you doing?" I answer. Then I get up from my desk, close, and lock the door, so there's no chance that Levi will come looking for me and interrupt this call.

"Things are good. Dale has some work in Savannah next week and I was hoping since I'll be going with him that maybe we can get together for lunch? I'd love to see Oakside."

Instantly I'm in a panic. I've always told her she should come down and check out Oakside. But what excuse could I possibly give her to keep her away, so she doesn't run into Levi?

Thinking quickly, I say, "I'd love to meet you for lunch. It's been a while since I've been in Savannah so maybe we could do a little shopping too?"

"Oh, I'd love that. I could really use some dresses as we go into summer and the warmer weather. Dale is really excited to see Oakside too, so we're going to set aside an entire day for it."

I had to stop myself from groaning. Any other time I would be ecstatic to show them around, but something in me didn't want to share Levi with her just yet. I feel like once they reconnect, they'll be no more reason for me to talk with him. Not sure why the thought of them reconnecting bothers me though. Something I'll have to dig into later.

"Actually, we're doing some construction here so we're not allowing visitors outside of those coming to see family. We just had a large donation, so we got right to work. We didn't want to waste time adding a few more rooms."

"Oh, that's great that you guys are doing so well! This won't be the last time that Dale is in Savannah as he picked up a new account there. Maybe next time we'll be able to take a tour."

I sag into my chair. Even though I hate lying to my friend, knowing that next time she should be able to tour makes me feel slightly better. She starts talking about everything that Dale is doing in Savannah, and a few of the restaurants they plan to eat at and my mind wanders.

"Why exactly did you and Levi break up?" I ask before I can really think to stop myself.

She laughs. "That was so long ago. Levi was a great guy but when he decided to go into the military instead of college, we talked, and even just between boot camp and training it would be months where we couldn't talk more than a few letters, and then after that we had no idea where he would be stationed. With me going off to college, it just seemed like the best idea."

"And if you hadn't broken up, you wouldn't have met Dale."

"Exactly. So I don't regret it."

"Did you keep in contact with him?" I ask, pushing my luck.

"I found him on Facebook about a year or so ago. He was stationed in Norfolk, VA, and getting ready to deploy again. But I haven't heard from him since. Why the sudden interest?"

Once again, thinking quickly on my feet, I feed her yet another lie. "We just got a guy in here that reminds me a lot of him, so I was just wondering."

When we wrap up the conversation, I hang up and finish my lunch before heading upstairs to check on Levi again. On my way, I think about talking to Lexi about my dilemma of not telling Rebecca that he's here. But I'm not sure I'm ready to talk about it to anyone, even though I know Lexi would gladly listen.

As I head into the lobby, she flags me down and I walk over to her.

"Maybe you can talk to Levi? He's refusing to go to his therapy session today. He doesn't have to go, but even if we could just find out what's wrong would be a start. If we knew how to assist him, it would be a huge help, and you are the one he's most likely to talk to."

This worries me, especially since he's been nothing but happy and perfectly adjusted to his new life. He hasn't mentioned anything that is upsetting or would cause this kind of a mood.

"I'll try, but he wouldn't even talk to me when I brought him food other than to say that he wanted to eat alone."

"Even that's not normal for him. Levi loves going into the dining room and interacting with people."

I nod and go to his room. Hesitating just outside the door, I try to think of what to say before taking a step into the room.

The door is cracked open like maybe a nurse had stuck their head in to talk to him and didn't close it all the way. Through the crack in the door, I can see Levi he's sitting in his chair in front of the same window he was at earlier, only this time he's silently crying into his hands. His shoulders are shaking, and the sight completely breaks my heart.

# Chapter 3

## Levi

I'm staring out the window with a million things running through my head when there's a knock on the door. I don't even turn to see who it is.

"Go away."

"You know it's okay to not be okay. You don't have to be strong all the time," Mandy says.

I hear them tell me this all the time around here, but it's hard to believe when you were taught something completely different growing up. Show no weakness. You have to be stronger than anything that comes at you, so it can't be used against you.

"No, it's not to my dad." Then I clamp my mouth shut as I've already let out more than I wanted to. What is it about this girl that has me opening up without even realizing what I'm doing?

"Why is that?" Mandy asks. When I turn to look at her, she's a few steps inside my room. Moving my chair around so I can face her, she takes a few more hesitant steps.

"My whole life growing up all he kept saying was show no weakness. He's a pro at it. He'd never show any emotion not even to my mother, my brother, or me. When I was on the honor roll for having straight A's, he never displayed any emotion, never told me he was proud. But he was great at letting you know when he was disappointed in you."

Yes, my father was a pro at punishing us. Once he caught me playing video games too late one night, and instead of taking away the video games, he turned off the Internet for the whole house. It didn't matter that I needed to do research the following day for a project that was due in just a few days. He simply told me to figure it out.

"When I joined the Army, his way of showing me that he was disappointed that I didn't want to take over the family business was to cut me off. And not just him. I haven't heard from my mom or my brother and I know that it's his doing. They're too scared to stand up to him."

Mandy doesn't say anything, but she looks like she's thinking as she takes a few more steps and then sits down on one of the leather chairs in my room. It's the chair that's furthest away from me, still giving me space. She sits on the edge of the chair, looking at her hands and then up at me.

"Is being like your dad what you want?"

"Fuck no, it's not! I don't want to be anything like him. That's why I joined the Army."

"Then it's okay to show weakness. They can see right through your act here and until you accept it, and have a breakdown, they won't release you. Even if you are running marathons."

She stands and grabs the plate from the food that I ate and turns to leave, but I suddenly don't want her to go.

"Will you stay? I really don't want to be alone right now."

She stops and looks at me for a moment and then gives me a soft smile.

"Give me five minutes. I have some cookies in my office."

• • • • ◉ • ◉ • • •

# Mandy

I hurried out of the room to find Lexi and Noah. Even though I feel a little bit like I'm betraying his trust, I know that they need all the information to be able to help him. If he finds out that I'm telling Lexi and Noah what he just told me, I just hope that he understands.

In order to have privacy, I asked them to join me in my office, and I relay everything that he just told me about his dad.

"I don't remember much about his father from when we were in school, but he always seemed like a cold person. Though no one really knew anything about him because he never talked to anybody," I tell Lexi and Noah.

"The best thing you can do is get him to talk to you. Doesn't matter what, even if it's something that might not seem like a big deal. Like the stuff with his father. But that could be what's holding him back. It's better for him to talk to anyone as opposed to no one," Lexi says.

"That's the plan," I say, agreeing. "He wants me to go back because he doesn't want to be alone right now. So hopefully this is a good sign that he's on the right path. Maybe he'll open up more after this."

I hesitate for a moment because I want to tell her about Rebecca, instead, I keep silent. Though I want someone to talk to about it, I don't think I'm ready to hear that I shouldn't have lied. Because if I'm honest with myself, I'm not quite sure why I did. Just the thought of them being together in the same room sets me on edge, and until I can work through my own feelings I don't think I'll be able to talk to anyone else about them.

After grabbing the cookies and my phone, I make sure that my computer is locked and go upstairs. I hesitate in his doorway unsure of what to do because he's back staring out the window. Shrugging my shoulders, I knock on the door frame and he turns to look at me over his shoulder. When he sees it's me, he moves his chair to face the seating area in his room like he was before.

Closing the door behind me, I sit in the chair that I was sitting at before, the one that is furthest away from him, giving him as much space as he wants.

"What do you have there?" he lifts his chin towards the Tupperware container that I placed on the coffee table.

"So fair warning, I stress bake. When I was up late last night, I made these new cookies.

I've never made them before so I'm not quite sure how they turned out. It's two cranberry cookies sandwiched together and in the middle is Nutella. It's a recipe I found online." I open the lid, offering him some. Wheeling over closer to me, he takes one from the container.

Then he looks over at me, then back at the cookie, and then back at me.

"What are you stressed about that you're stress baking?"

Maybe I shouldn't have told him that because I'm not ready to tell him that I'm stressing over Rebecca wanting to come and visit, and whether I want her to see him again. Maybe if I'm vague enough, he'll let it go. I guess if he pushes, I can always push him to talk and that should get him to drop it.

"I just have a few things going on with a friend," I tell him, keeping it as vague as possible.

"Do you want to talk about it? I'm a good listener."

"I don't know. Do you want to talk about all that's going on with your dad right now?" I ask, staring him down.

He holds my stare as he takes a few bites of the cookie before he nods.

"Fair enough. I'll drop it."

"So, tell me about once you joined the Army," I say, racking my brain for anything to change the subject. His eyes go dark, and I almost wonder if he's not going to answer me.

"Or you can talk about high school," I say, giving him an out if he doesn't want to talk about his military time.

"Well, you already know that my dad was strict. I knew from an early age I didn't want to grow up to be like him, but somehow, I let him steer me into applying to business schools so that I could eventually take over the family business. There was a moment at prom that it all became crystal clear that it was not what I wanted."

He clamps his lips together and looks away from me as if he said something he thinks I might not want to hear.

"What is it?"

"I don't know if I should say this since you're still friends with Rebecca."

"We don't talk all that much now that she is married and I haven't seen her in over a year. Though she's making plans to be in Savannah and wants me to come down for lunch."

He stares out the window, thinking. I realize that he may not want to tell me, and he might be trying to figure out how to switch the subject. Right then, I decide I'm not going to push and I only want him to talk about what he wants to talk about. I want him to be comfortable talking to me.

"Honestly, I'm sure you know that Rebecca and I lost our virginity to each other on prom night. She told you everything, so I'm not going to pretend that you don't know that. That night she started talking about our future and where she saw us in five to ten years since we were supposed to go to the same college together. When she started talking about me working with my father, I realized that was the absolute last thing I wanted."

"I knew you went your separate ways, but she never told me what you guys talked about. The only thing she said was it was personal. There were some lines that as friends we just never crossed."

"The next morning, I took her home and went straight down to the recruiter's office. I knew that there was no way I could choose another college or change my degree and that this would be the only way to get away from my dad. After I signed the contract that day, there would be no way he could force me out of it. I needed a permanent kind of way of getting out from underneath him."

"Rebecca told me she tried to be understanding, but even though she never really said it, I feel like she thought that she said something that pushed you towards it," I say.

"In a way she did, but it wasn't her fault. It was mine for not standing up to my dad sooner. I didn't tell him right away what I had done, and two days before graduation is when he found out. He discovered the signed contract in my room. For the next two days, he would not leave me alone, telling me that I needed to get out of it, that I couldn't do it because I had already committed to college and him. I have never been so relieved as to go to school for graduation that day."

"That's also the day that you and Rebecca broke up. I told her not to do it at graduation, but she said that she needed a clean break. Since graduating was the end of high school, then it should also be the end of her high school relationship."

"I can honestly agree with her there. Her breaking up with me was exactly what I needed at the time. After graduation, I started packing my bags and my dad threatened to cut me off. Then I just shrugged, packed my bags, and left. My recruiter let me stay on his couch for two days before he took me to the bus. That was the last time I heard from my dad, my mom, or my brother. They never sent letters, emails, or care packages and I stopped sending them forwarding addresses."

"If you decide you want to reach out to your brother or your mom, Noah and Lexi are more than happy to help you contact them."

# Chapter 4

## Levi

Why am I even telling her this? I'm not sure, but for some reason, I just can't stop talking to her.

"My brother has been working to take over the business, at least from what I've read online and seen shared from various friends who I still keep in contact with."

It's hard to watch my family's life like I'm an outsider, but I know even if I stayed there, I couldn't have taken over the company. There is no going back now. I made my choice and know even though my career in the military might be over, there is no going home either.

I haven't wanted to think much about it, but I need to figure out not just my next steps but what those next steps are going to be.

She holds out the container of cookies to me, and I take another one. These cookies are really good, better than anything I've ever had, either from the store or even the bake sales the school used to do.

As I take a bite, I remember what she said about stress baking. Something in me hates the cookies as much as I like them. They're exceptionally good, and I could eat the entire container of them, but I hate that they were made from her stress.

When she still hasn't said anything about my comments about my family, I decide to switch up the subject. The atmosphere seems to be getting a little too heavy.

"These cookies really are good, better than anything I've ever had. You could probably win some awards in the baking contests back home."

"No way. Those competitions are too cutthroat, and those old ladies are so serious about those ribbons I wouldn't dare even enter. Much less try to win anything."

"Yeah, they might come and dig all your flowers up."

"Or run you over with a car."

We both smile, and it's then I find I want to know more about her.

"Now that you know all about mine, tell me about your family."

When we were in school, I don't remember hearing anything about her family. Rebecca never mentioned it, and never hung out at her house. Mandy was always hanging out at Rebecca's house and always seemed reluctant to go home. I never thought much of it then, but now I wonder if that was a sign of not-so-great home life.

Mandy seems uncomfortable as she straightens a few of the car magazines that are on the coffee table in front of her.

"Nothing to tell, really. I didn't have any family and bounced around from one foster home to another until I aged out. Though I was lucky to be able to stay in the same school district. Many foster kids aren't that fortunate. But I stayed out of the way of my foster parents and they left me alone. I got a full scholarship, and then I was out of there."

It's like a punch to the gut knowing that she didn't have anyone. My family wasn't the best, but I knew that they would always be there if I needed them. Though she seemed pretty good at keeping it to herself because no one in school knew. I wonder if Rebecca even knew, but I figure it's not the time to ask.

"What was your major in college?"

"I wanted to run a company, but I wasn't sure about what kind. What I did know is that I wanted to be my own boss, because I was so tired of people telling me what to do with every aspect of my life. About halfway through school, I changed gears to help with charities."

"That's a huge shift. What caused the change?"

I know I'm prying into her life, but it's a hell of a lot easier and safer than trying to pry into mine. And if I keep her on this track, maybe she'll leave my family and everything out of it.

"One of the classes I took as a requirement was to shadow some business people and see what all the aspects of a company were like. The one I selected, the CEO was also a woman, and she was very big on her charity projects, and explained to me why giving back to the community was so important."

She stops and smiles, looking out the window getting a faraway look in her eye before continuing.

"A few weeks later, I went back and asked her about the different charity projects she was working on, and she took me with her. It was working hands-on with some children who were in an orphanage. That was the first time I realized that it could have been a lot worse for me. When I told her my story, she was the first person I really talked to about it, and she reminded me I knew where these kids are coming from more than anyone, and I could help them."

She opens her mouth like she's going to keep talking and then clamps it shut. I want her to keep talking because I want to know what she was going to say because it seems to be important.

"And?"

"And I kept coming back to the orphanage, and I continued to volunteer there for the rest of the time that I was in school. The entire experience changed me and that's why I changed gears. In my senior year of school, I wanted to get some experience, and Lexi and Noah were just starting this up. They didn't have money to hire someone, so I volunteered in exchange for the hours that I needed for my final class, showing that I was working with a charity. The rest is history. Our first event did really well, and they hired me full-time after that."

"So, what exactly do you do here? You said you're the charity coordinator?"

She smiles and shakes her head.

"That's my official title, but because we are still such a small organization, we are all wearing many hats. My main job is to organize events to raise money for the charity, to help get the word out, and find donors. We've got a few businessmen that are on-call to sponsor someone who may not have the insurance to cover themselves but need to be here. Basically, I'm in charge of any event that brings in money."

"What other hats do you wear?"

I just want to keep her talking because something about her voice is soothing all the demons inside of me. This was a day that started off as one that I wanted to sleep away and not deal with, but her simply talking to me, it's now a day that I can face.

"Since I'm the one that brings in most of the money here, I help with a lot of the budgeting; trying to figure out the best places to spend it. We've done pretty well with our events, and we just finished fixing up the barn. Now we're working on bringing in horses for equine therapy. Then we'll need the right people to manage the barn, a few ranch hands to do the grunt work, equine therapists, and since we're going to have animals we need to have a vet at least on call. So, I've been the one lining all that up."

"I heard talk of a possible swimming pool?"

"Not just a swimming pool. Lexi, Noah, and I have big dreams of an entire Aquatic Center. It would include an Olympic size swimming pool for laps, and a smaller pool that you can wade into that will help take the weight off of an injury, a hot tub, a sauna, and even one of those pools that you're swimming in place, and you can increase the resistance against the waves you're swimming against. That last one is not cheap."

She laughs, but I get the feeling that no matter the cost, she'll make it happen. When she pauses, I again have this need to keep her talking.

"Aren't there grants for places like this?"

"Oh, there are, but I don't know the first thing about grants. Lexi has a friend's daughter who's taking care of the grants. She doesn't actually work here on the property, but she does a lot of it at home. Apparently, her dad was killed in action like Lexi's husband was."

It takes me a minute to digest those words. It's never easy to hear about losing a military member. But did she just say that Lexi's husband was killed in action? Isn't Lexi's husband, Noah?

"But isn't Noah Lexi's husband?" I ask, needing an answer.

She smiles softly and then looks down for a moment before she answers.

"After Lexi married her high school sweetheart, he enlisted in the Marines. His name was Tyler, and he was killed in his second deployment. There's a plaque in the lobby by the stairs that has his photo, with his flag folded in a shadowbox. On the plaque, there's some information about him. Lexi met Noah when her brother was injured, and Noah has made it a point to keep Tyler very included in Oakside."

I know it's every wife's greatest fear to get the phone call that their husband was killed. Heck, it's every family member's greatest fear. Though I doubt it was my father's. I know my mother and my brother would be upset, hell, my mother would be devastated. But I have to wonder if my father would even attend my funeral. The dark mood from earlier seems to be settling back over me. But Mandy doesn't notice.

"Lexi is so full of life you would never know everything she's been through. But they are the only family that I have now, and she treats me like I'm a blood relative. It's almost like what I would imagine having a sister would be like. Her dad and brother helped when I was doing some renovations on my house, and it was great to have someone look over my shoulder and make sure everything was done correctly."

She shakes her head and abruptly stands up.

"But I'm sure all this is the last thing you want to talk about. Sorry that I've taken up so much of your time."

"Mandy," I say with as much authority as I can muster.

It takes a minute before her eyes land back on me.

"I'd like to think that we're friends. Are we not friends?"

She sighs and starts biting on the corner of her lip, a move that draws my eye, and I can't turn away from it.

"Yes. Yes, Levi, we're friends."

"Good. Then you're not wasting my time. Friends talk. We get to know each other better and that's what we're doing. As crazy as it sounds, having you here talking took my mind off of everything, and I think I needed that." At least for the last part.

Though I'm looking down at my hands in my lap, I can feel her eyes on me. I try not to let it show, but in general, having anyone's eyes on me since the accident makes me uncomfortable. It doesn't matter if it's my doctor, nurse, or any of the guys here. I know it's something I have to deal with, and I will, or I guess I should say, I am at least trying.

When I finally look up at her, she offers me a smile and I feel like I just won the lottery.

"At the risk of sounding like your doctors and probably everyone else here, talking always helps, even if it's not about what is actually bothering you. Taking your mind off of a situation can be more powerful than you realize."

She pauses for a minute, and I'm stunned by the realization that she's right.

"I have tomorrow off and then I will be getting ready for some interviews that I have lined up for Lexi, Noah, and Easton. So, I'll be a little busy, but I will try to bring you some more home-cooked meals if you promise to at least start talking to your therapist, even if it's not about your time in the military. Deal?"

Why do I have this need in my gut to please her and to make her happy? And it's not about the food, which is a huge bonus because they serve healthy stuff here. It's good food, but it's not exactly the kind of stuff that you crave after months of being out in the desert.

No, I don't want to, but I have this need to make her smile more, and I'm not sure what to make of it, but I find myself nodding and agreeing before I even realize what I'm doing. That earns me another smile and I know in that moment I would do anything for that smile.

Too bad that smile is going to get me into more trouble than I had bargained for.

# Chapter 5

## Mandy

Its been a week since my talk with Levi and he kept his promise. The next day when he went to his appointment with his therapist he started talking. I'm not sure about what and I won't ask him because that's between him and Doctor Tate, but at least he's talking.

Lexi and Noah were so stunned that they called me on my day off, which they never do. They wanted to know what my secret was, and how I got him to talk. I told them that I just bribed him with food, and they laughed. Lexi joked about bribing all their patients to go to their appointments and do what they're supposed to do. But Noah put an end to that real quick.

Today is a day of interviews set up to get more exposure out there for Oakside. From the beginning, we've always been very big on letting the community know what we're doing, what our plans are, and where we're going.

Though southern Georgia isn't a huge military area, we are in a military town. We aren't too far away from the Marine training area on Parris Island, South Carolina. We are a day's drive to the Navy hub at Norfolk, Virginia. It's only a few hours' drive to the Navy station in Jacksonville, Florida. And there are a good fifteen Army bases within a day's drive of us.

So, we've always made it a point to be very public about what we're doing and our plans. The community has been generous with donations and helping out. Right now, we have more volunteers than we need. Which is a very good problem to have.

Since the weather is absolutely beautiful today, we've decided to set up the interviews on the front lawn, so that the background is of Oakside. We have six different interviews lined up, and three of them are video interviews. While the weather is still nice, we'll do them first, and then the other three will be in several major newspapers in the area and will include photos.

We're getting set up, and the closer we get to the interview time, the more agitated Noah gets. He doesn't like being the center of attention, and it's no wonder. He was injured in action and was burned quite badly. After the explosion, the entire right side of his body was covered in burns. Though he had some plastic surgery done on his face, there are still scars you can see along his neck and on his hand. As a result, he mostly wears long pants and long sleeves.

Lexi knows how to calm him, and he's just holding her to him as if she might run away. Their love is intense and something that I have loved to watch. They've been so good for each other, but they're even better together.

Easton is just as irritated, but fortunately, his wife Paisley is here. She's helping keep him calm, and his dog Allie is also doing her best to keep him relaxed. Easton was in the first round of patients here at Oakside. During his time in the hospital, no one met him.

For just over a year, Easton was a prisoner of war. He was tortured repeatedly, and he isn't fond of talking about that time, but he's agreed to do it today because it's going to help the men and women here at Oakside.

He too has his arms around Paisley and at his side is Allie who is sitting and resting her head on his leg just enough to let him know that she's there. I got to watch Easton and Paisley's love story unfold in a front-row seat. Paisley is Easton's best friend's little sister. Apparently, they had a crush on each other growing up, but neither of them acted on it.

Lexi met Paisley at the hospital when she would bring her dog Molly in to work with the patients. Though Lexi had no idea that Paisley and Easton knew each other, and neither of them knew that the other one was at Oakside until Molly brought them together. After that, Paisley was who Easton wanted to get better for.

As Easton was getting closer to his discharge, Noah offered him a job running the security here. He took it, and Paisley still volunteers her time with Molly and continues to train service dogs for the men and women at Oakside.

Both of these couple's stories are exactly what needs to be shared. Letting people into their personal lives isn't easy, but they're willing to do it for Oakside.

Each interview is going to be set up a little differently, but this one has a large wicker couch that was taken from one of the porches at Oakside, and both couples are sitting on it. Allie is sitting at Easton's feet, and the beautiful southern antebellum home that is now Oakside is featured behind them.

Lexi seems to take the lead in the interview. She and Paisley are fearless when it comes to raising awareness for the service members at Oakside. Even though this is a video interview, it's going on a big military website and also on a few social media sites. They asked all the standard questions about how Oakside came to be.

They want to know how Noah and Lexi met, about Easton's time as a patient, and they ask about Paisley and Easton's relationship. Then they move into the part that everyone's been dreading. The part where Noah tells his story of how he got his scars, and Easton is going to talk about his time as a prisoner of war.

I've heard both their stories before, but every time I do it's still gut-wrenching. You can't listen to Easton talk about being tortured for a year in a room without sunlight and not have tears in your eyes.

Well, most people probably have their focus on the men that are talking, but I can't take my eyes off of Lexi and Paisley. They're right there supporting their guys, holding their hands and rubbing their arms, letting them know that it's good to tell their stories and that they're right there for them.

Until I came here, I never really had a role model of what a good, healthy marriage looks like. Outside of romantic movies and romance novels, I didn't know what it was like to find the partner that makes you better. But watching these two couples together, I know that this is what I want.

It makes dating pretty hard because I'm picky. I guess it's why I've recently stopped dating, and focused so much energy on Oakside. But now I'm looking forward more and more to spending time with Levi. I enjoy coming to work because I know I'll get to see him. Then I know my lunchtime will be fun because I'll get to sit down and eat with him.

Even though right now we're just friends, I can't help but feel like it's more. But I won't ever bring that up and chance ruining what we have.

I'm pulled from going down that train of thought as this interview wraps up and everyone starts moving around. The next group of people that will do an interview want to focus more on Oakside and what we have coming up, so it'll be a much lighter interview. They start setting up, and Lexi walks over to me and wraps an arm around my waist pulling me to her side.

"What's on your mind? I could tell that you were a million miles away from here." Lexi keeps her arm around my waist, moving me away from the crowd.

"Just me wishing yet again that I had the type of relationship that you have, or that Paisley and Easton seemed to have found. Until I met all of you, I didn't know that type of commitment and bond existed, at least not outside of a romance novel. But now I crave it."

"Well, things with you and Levi seem to be getting pretty serious. You're spending a lot of time together, is there anything there?"

"No, we're just friends. Besides, he dated my high school best friend, so I think that technically makes him off-limits," I finally admit to her. I tried to shake it off like it's not a big deal, but for some reason, it feels like it is a big deal.

"Wait, you mean your friend Rebecca?"

"Yeah, they were together in high school, went to prom and all that jazz." I try to wave it off, but of course, Lexi isn't going to drop it.

"She's married now with a kid on the way. I think that kind of makes the pact of her ex being off-limits void, don't you?"

"So, you're telling me that you'd be okay with me dating one of your exes?"

"Yes. I love Noah, and there are absolutely no feelings left for any of my exes. I do love Tyler but that is different. Not that there really are any ex-boyfriends. There were a few dates, but outside of that, there wasn't really anyone serious."

It just feels like I'm breaking some kind of girl code and I don't want to keep talking about it. Thankfully, Lexi seems to sense this but isn't quite finished.

"You should just talk to Rebecca, even if nothing comes of it, at least then you're covered. But you have to do what feels right for you, and I'll drop it now," she says just as Noah walks up and pulls her to his side.

"Drop what?" Noah asks.

"Something that we're done talking about, but I'm sure she will fill you in on all of it tonight." I smile and wink at them.

Noah and Lexi don't have any secrets. They tell each other everything and don't hide the fact that they do. That's how I know their relationship is going to work.

The next interview begins, and they hit all the talking points I gave them about where the barn is, and our plans for the Aquatic Center that we want to start working towards next. They talk about the benefits of having the different kinds of therapy, from letting the patients work in the garden to riding and caring for horses.

After going over all the advantages of having an Aquatic Center, and how much progress we've made, they go on to give examples of some current and former patients that the Aquatic Center would be good for without actually giving away their names.

The interviewer asks about Allie and how Easton's working with his therapy dog. In turn, Easton talks about Paisley and how she's working with them.

Then the interviewer asks us a question that none of us are ready for.

"Where do you see yourselves and Oakside in the next ten years? Especially if you had the funding that you needed and were able to do whatever you wanted."

Lexi and Noah look at each other, and then she looks over at me. I just shrug because we haven't had this conversation, so she's flying blind here. Lexi then looks back at the interviewer and smiles.

"I honestly haven't had this conversation with any of my staff or even my husband. But if money wasn't an issue, I would love to start opening up other branches of Oakside across the country. We would focus on heavy military areas around military bases. As far as I know, there's only one other place like this, and there should be many, many more."

Immediately, my mind starts swirling with the possibilities. Of course, money is always going to be an obstacle. But with the right planning, after we get the Aquatic Center set up, we could focus on scholarships to help soldiers that need assistance, but insurance won't cover them. Particularly the ones who have been out of the military for a while now and could use our help.

Or we could begin planning for the next place that we want to open. We won't be able to do it as cheaply as we did Oakside, because Lexi had owned this home beforehand. But with the right planning, I think that we could make it happen. Maybe at least one more place within the next ten years.

Just like that, Lexi's dream has become mine. Looking over at Easton and Paisley, I can see the dream is starting to take root in their minds as well. She just put it out to the universe, and knowing the team that we have here, well, we will make it happen.

# Chapter 6

## Levi

The interviews that Mandy helped with last week have been drawing a lot of attention to Oakside. I know that was the plan and I've been watching the videos and reading the articles. The team here is completely dedicated to the soldiers.

Mandy had this idea of capitalizing on the attention that we were getting by starting a pen pal program. People could write the soldiers that are healing at Oakside, so they didn't feel quite so alone.

Many of them get visitors, family, friends, or even people from their unit. But there are many like me who don't have any visitors. And if it weren't for Mandy, I don't think I would be as far along in my treatment as I am.

Sometimes having someone to talk to you and treat you like you're normal goes a long way. In many cases, even further than therapy can take you.

Every day that she works, Mandy's been having lunch with me. She checks to make sure I've been going to all of my appointments. Even though my nurse always confirms and encourages me to go to appointments, it's different when you have a friend cheering you on. Especially someone that you don't want to disappoint.

The highlight of my days here is Mandy visiting me. She's always trying new cookie recipes and bringing them in, and now she's been delivering me home-cooked lunches.

Today's lunch looks like meatloaf sandwiches. I remember my mom always cooked two meatloaves when she would make it for dinner, and then the next day, we would have meatloaf sandwiches just like these. When I was stateside, they would make meatloaf sandwiches at the mess hall, but they were barely edible. If you were lucky, they were only too bland. Otherwise, it was like they dumped the whole spice cabinet in the meat.

We're about halfway through lunch and have already covered all the topics, like making sure I went to my appointment and what she's been working on today. For the last few minutes, we've been eating in silence, and she keeps looking up at me like she has something to say but doesn't want to bring it up.

Sighing, I finally set my sandwich down. "Whatever it is, just say it, and let's get it over with so I can enjoy my lunch," I say, trying to get her to talk. But she still looks hesitant.

"Okay so, don't be mad." she cringes as she says it.

Setting my plate on the coffee table in front of me, I brace myself for news that I know I'm not going to like, maybe something that's probably going to make me mad.

"People don't start a conversation like that unless they did something they know they shouldn't have done, and they know the other person is going to be mad. So let's get this over with," I hold my hands in my lap and stare her down waiting for her to admit whatever she did.

She's quiet for a moment, either scared to tell me or trying to figure out how to explain whatever it is. In that time, a million possibilities race through my head.

"Well, you know the pen pal program I told you that we were starting up?"

Nodding, I encourage her to go on.

"We've had an overwhelming amount of people sign up wanting to write soldiers who are here. But there weren't many here at Oakside who signed up to get a pen pal, so, I signed you up for one." She pulls an envelope from her purse and hands it to me.

Hesitating, I reach across the coffee table and take it from her, and set it in my lap without touching it.

"I'm sorry! Even though I know I should have told you or talked to you first about it, but you're one of the people here that doesn't have any visitors. And I wanted you to have someone to talk to and someone else to interact with."

When I hear the words coming out of my mouth, I don't realize that it's actually me speaking them. It's as if my brain is on autopilot.

"You're right, you should have talked to me. There was a reason I didn't sign up. Did you ever think about that? Not everyone wants to spill the details about why they're here or about all the sad stories in our lives. Because trust me, everyone that's here has plenty of sob stories. The fact that soldiers didn't sign up should have been your hint that this wasn't a good idea, and you should have put an end to it instead of dragging us into it."

Her eyes mist over, but she keeps her composure. Then stands up, takes her purse, plate and containers.

"Again, I said I was sorry. What you do with the letter and your pen pal is up to you. Trust me, I won't interfere again." Her voice is shaky, but she doesn't say anything else as she turns around and walks out.

Tossing the letter onto the coffee table, I wheel myself over to the window that I like to look out. The window has a view of the front lawn and down the long tree-lined driveway.

I don't know how long I sit there, but eventually, my nurse knocks on the door frame. I look over my shoulder to acknowledge her before turning to the back out the window.

"I know you're having a bad day, but I still have to check on you. Do you need anything? Are you in any pain?"

"How do you know that I'm not having a good day?"

"Well, generally, when you sit in that spot and stare out the window you do it when you're in one of your moods. When you're having a bad day. On your good days, you're reading, watching TV, or you're even out in the lobby interacting with people."

Turning to look over my shoulder at her, I wonder how she knows me so well. I'm almost certain Mandy told her to check on me because that's the only explanation that makes sense.

"We're trained to read our patients and figure out what their mannerisms mean," she says like she can read my mind.

I sigh and turn my chair to face her.

"Are you sure it wasn't Mandy telling you to check up on me?" I snap at her, but she doesn't even flinch.

"No, she didn't ask me to check on you but I did notice she was upset leaving your room. So, I made the decision myself to come and see if you need to talk or even yell at someone. I'm here if you want to," she says, her voice steady, not reacting to my anger.

Her calm demeanor seems to be exactly what I need to diffuse the anger that I couldn't seem to get rid of on my own.

"I'm sorry Kaitlyn. You didn't deserve that. Mandy and I did have a disagreement but she didn't need to be snapped at either. So, I guess you're right, I am having a bad day and just didn't realize it myself."

"That's par for the course here. You're going through a lot of changes and on anyone that's hard, but it's even harder on the soldiers here who have been through a traumatic event such as you. It's all right to have bad days, and we know that there are days you're going to snap at us. But when you come out the other side, make sure you apologize to those who took a beating from you during that time."

Then she turns, walking back down the hallway, and I know she's talking about Mandy. Since Mandy doesn't normally work with patients, maybe she wasn't as good as Kaitlyn is at hiding her emotions when people snap at her.

I start to feel bad about how I treated her, and I'm debating what to do about it when I see the letter that she handed me sitting on the coffee table.

Wheeling myself over, I pick up the letter. Looks to be a man's handwriting, and the address is from some town in North Carolina called Seaview. I've never heard of it before. Carefully opening the letter, I pull out the two pieces of paper inside.

One paper has a drawing that looks like it was drawn by a little kid. It's done in crayon and shows a man and a little boy standing next to a soldier. There is a huge American flag flying overhead, and he even drew grass, sky, clouds, and the sun. I set the picture down in my lap and focus on the letter inside.

*Levi,*

*When I heard about the soldier pen pal program, I felt compelled to put my name on the list. I'm not sure why, but I did.*

*My name is Kade, and the drawing is from my son. Okay, if I'm being honest, it's probably ninety percent from my wife and ten percent from my son, since he's only three years old right now.*

*The paperwork we got with your address mentioned how you are going through a big life change between your injury, your military time, and transferring to civilian life.*

*I know it's not quite the same, but a few years ago I had a dramatic life change myself. One that was forced on me, and I know it's not easy to deal with when you have a life plan and everything comes crashing down. Re-planning your entire life sucks.*

*There's no better word for it. Just sucks.*

*See, in my previous life I lived in California. Then a series of events that I had no control over made it so it was 'suggested' that I take a break and regroup. I was sent here to Seaview in North Carolina.*

*Now, this isn't a bad place to be exiled to. I had a room right on the beach, the food here is delicious, and the people are really friendly.*

*But I felt this need to prove I wasn't who they thought I was and in doing so, I did it with a fake relationship. That relationship was the best thing and the worst thing I ever did. That woman is now my wife, but we started on very rocky terms. Because we were both convinced that it was just a fake relationship, when the opportunity came, I went back to California.*

*Even though I was convinced I could just step back into my old life, it only took me a couple of days to realize that I wasn't that person anymore. Sure, I could go back to that life and fake it 'til I make it, but it wasn't what I wanted anymore.*

*Before I could move forward, I had to admit that to myself. Then I could come back out here and admit it to my now wife. But in doing so, I've never been happier, and I don't even want to think of what my life would have been if I had stayed in California.*

*All this to say. Right now, things can look bad. Like there's no way you can have a life without the life you previously had. But if you were to go back today, everything would be different.*

*My wife wants me to make sure I tell you that you are at a point that many people never get to experience. The point where you can go anywhere and do anything you want. You have to pick a path and don't have anything preventing you from starting over. She said to embrace the change. It's going to be scary, but it'll be worth it.*

*If nothing else, I hope you will choose to write us back. So my wife doesn't think I scared you off. Above all else, thank you for your service, thank you for your sacrifice, and I'm sorry for those that you lost.*

*Kade Markson*

Until I run my hands over my eyes, I don't realize I have tears running down my face. I hadn't thought about those that I lost in the blast until just now. I've been pushing them to the back of my mind.

Taking a moment, I read the letter over again. This time it's the signature that catches my attention. Kade Markson was a megastar Hollywood actor with a playboy reputation. I don't remember much of the story, but I do remember the guys that I was stationed with telling me that he met some girl and gave it all up and settled down.

There's no way that this is the same guy, right?

I take the letter over to my desk and write him back.

*Kade,*

*You're one of the lucky ones that found the woman you're meant to be with. I've talked to a few guys that have completed their treatment here and many of them say that the love of a woman is a powerful motivator for healing.*

*Unfortunately, I don't have that. I don't even have my family. They didn't approve of my decision to join the Army. The only good thing to come out of all this is one of the girls that works here was best friends with my high school girlfriend.*

*It's been nice to catch up with her and talk about old times.*

*You are right, there is no going back. I lost part of my leg, so I was honorably and medically discharged. I'm just trying to take one day at a time, but thinking about starting an entirely new life outside the walls of Oakside is scary as hell.*

*But I have to ask if you're the same Kade Markson that was the Hollywood actor. Much of the story sounds the same. It seems like a few of the guys that I was stationed with overseas followed your story when it happened.*

*Either way, I appreciate the encouraging words and I hope that you will keep writing. I'm one of the few here that doesn't get any visitors. So, it's nice to talk to someone in the outside world.*

*Levi*

Putting the letter in an envelope, I address it and then take it to Mandy who I'm sure is in her office.

Sure enough, she's sitting at her desk. When I tap on the door frame to get her attention, she looks up but doesn't say anything.

"I'm sorry for snapping at you. I didn't realize that I was having a bad day until my nurse pointed it out. Regardless, I shouldn't have taken it out on you. I wish I could say it would be the last time, but I can't promise that, but I can promise I will do my best to try to recognize my bad days before they get this far again."

She nods, giving me a small smile.

"I know it happens, and it's not the first time a patient has gone off on me. But it's the first time I considered that patient a friend. So, I guess I took it a bit harder than I should have. All is forgiven."

Something in my gut screams that she is putting me in the patient and friend category, but I let it go for now.

I hold up the letter to Kade and wheel forward to set it on her desk.

"I wrote my pen pal back."

Her blinding smile I receive in return sets my heart racing, and for the first time since my injury, my cock gets hard.

# Chapter 7

## Mandy

For whatever reason, I couldn't sleep last night, so I decided to get up and go into work early. I guess the fight with Levi was bothering me more than I expected it to. Even sitting at my desk, I found it hard to concentrate, and kept wondering if Levi was awake, was he eating breakfast, and if he was eating in his room or in the dining room.

I feel like a schoolgirl who wants to go see her crush, but I don't want to seem overeager like a stalker either. This is going to be a problem. For one, he's a patient, even though he's not my patient.

Then there's the fact that I work here, and he's a patient here. It's almost like a forbidden office romance. He's here to heal and I'm here to work, which I have to keep reminding myself. Add in the mixture of guilt I feel about not telling Rebecca that he's here, and not talking to Levi about Rebecca Well, it's just a bad situation.

Finally deciding I need to talk to someone so that I can clear my mind and get some work done, I go hunt for Lexi.

After I check her office downstairs and find it empty, I figure she's upstairs talking to people, or trying to get work finished before everyone wakes up. But I know she's here because a few months ago Noah insisted on getting a golf cart for them to drive from their house next door to Oakside. When I got in, that golf cart was sitting outside the side door.

Going upstairs, I peek into the dining room, thinking maybe she's sitting and eating with someone. Though I don't see her, Levi's sitting in the corner. When he spots me, he waves me over. I hate admitting to myself, but I was hoping that he would be here, and it's why I started with the dining room.

"I don't normally see you here this early," Levi says.

"Yeah, I need to talk to Lexi. You haven't seen her, have you?"

"Everything okay?"

"Yes, I just came in early to get some work done, and have a question for her." Even though I hate lying to him, there is no way I can tell him the real reason I need to find her.

"I haven't seen her, but I saw Noah when he peeked in here about fifteen minutes ago and then left with some food."

"Well, he wasn't downstairs, so he's probably out on the back porch. I wonder if they're eating breakfast out there. I'll go check. Thank you. Make sure you go to your doctor's appointment today, and I'll have cookies waiting for you at lunch."

That gets a smile out of him, which sends my heart racing. When I smile at him, our eyes lock, and neither of us moves. We stay locked in each other's gaze for what feels like hours, but I know isn't more than a minute before someone clears their throat.

When I look up, there's another patient who looks like he wants to sit down and talk to Levi, so I get up and with another smile leave the dining room.

Then I go to the back porch, and just like I was expecting Noah is out there eating with one of the patients.

"Noah, I don't want to interrupt, but do you happen to know where Lexi is? I need to talk to her about something."

"She's still back at the house. When she didn't sleep well last night, I let her sleep in. Is everything okay?"

"Yeah, it's more of a personal matter. Is it all right if I go over there and check on her? It's not like her to not be here by now."

He reaches into his pocket and pulls out a small key ring, and hands it to me.

"Yeah, take the golf cart. With how tired she's been, I don't want her walking. There's a house key on there as well."

Since I started working at Oakside, I've become good friends with Lexi and Noah to the point that they have me over to dinner several times a month. When I knock on the door, they've started to get mad that I don't walk in.

The last time I was over for dinner I knocked and got a lecture about how I'm family, and family doesn't need to knock. When I followed up with how I don't want to walk into something that I can't unsee, they laughed. Then they said when they know that I'm coming they can restrain themselves. But for me it was a little awkward, yet it's completely Lexi and Noah.

Getting in the golf cart, I drive down the large paved sidewalk that Lexi had Noah put in. It goes from Oakside to their side door and cuts through the trees that separate Oakside property from the property their house is on. They really did this pathway up nice as there are plenty of lights at night and several benches where you can sit down and relax. But you can't see their house or Oakside, and you feel like you're all alone in the area.

Lexi has plans in a few months to plant flowers along the edges to bring some color to the area. Right now, there are just a few small patches of wildflowers.

Parking the golf cart in the driveway, I walk up to the front porch and knock on the door. But when I look through the side window, I don't see any movement and the downstairs looks pretty dark. When I test the door, I find it's unlocked, so I go in and lock the door behind me.

Figuring maybe she isn't even out of bed yet, I go upstairs. When I get to their room, the bathroom light is on and the door is cracked open.

"Lexi, are you alright? Noah said you didn't get a lot of sleep last night."

"Mandy, thank God. I thought it was Noah coming to check on me. Can you come in here?"

Hesitantly, I walk to the door and look in. Lexi is sitting on the floor next to the toilet with her back to the cabinets. Other than looking a little pale, she's otherwise okay. Sitting down on the floor across from her, I put my back to the wall.

"Are you okay? You sure you don't want me to go get Noah?"

Lexi gives me a small smile and shakes her head.

"I've been sick and trying to hide it from him. Actually, I'm glad you're here because I need your help."

Internally, I start to panic. If Noah knew that she was sick, he wouldn't leave her side. But if he finds out that I know she's sick and didn't tell him, he'll be furious. Lexi is his life, and she always comes first. There isn't anything that man wouldn't do for her.

"You know I can't keep this kind of a secret from him. Even if it turned out you were perfectly fine in a few days, he would kill me."

"Calm down. I'm not sick because of a virus. It's morning sickness." She points to the counter above her.

When I stand, I can see on the back of the counter there are two pregnancy tests.

How I missed them when I first came in, I don't know. I guess I was more focused because I found Lexi on the floor. Taking a step closer, I can see both of them say positive.

"You're pregnant?"

"Yes. The morning sickness hit yesterday, and I hadn't realized that I missed my period until then."

Sitting back down on the floor with my back once again to the wall, I stare at Lexi.

"You won't be able to hide this from him forever. Sometimes he knows you better than you know yourself."

"I know, and I plan to tell him either today or tomorrow. But when he was injured, there was a point where his doctors were unsure if he'd ever be able to have kids. So, I want to do something to really celebrate this moment. It could be a fluke for all we know. Will you help me?"

"Of course, I'll help! What do you need?"

"First, I need you to go to the store and get me some crackers, ginger ale, and anything that you can find for morning sickness. All I want to do is hide this from him long enough to plan a surprise. While you're gone, I'll hop online and look up different ways to tell him."

"All right, I'll head out now. But we need a cover story because I had to ask him where you were, and he was the one that told me I'd find you here."

"Hey, wait a minute. What did you need? Is everything okay?" Leave it to Lexi to still worry about everyone else, even when she's not feeling great.

"I kind of need some advice on something, but it can wait. I want to make sure that you're settled and feeling better first."

"Well, that's the perfect excuse. I'll text him and say that you need some girl time, so I'll be late coming in today. If you take my car and keep the garage closed, he won't even know you're gone."

I hesitate for only a moment before I agree.

"Fine. But if we get caught and this blows up in our faces, I'm totally throwing you under the bus."

That gets a little chuckle out of her and she starts to look a lot better than when I first got here.

Once at the store, I get the things Lexi asked for. The woman at the counter also suggests these lollipops that are supposed to help with morning sickness, so I pick up a couple of bags of those as well. At this point, I'll get anything to try to keep her secret for at least twenty-four hours.

When I get back to Lexi's place, she's downstairs on the couch with a large kitchen pot sitting on the coffee table.

"Well, at least this looks better than that hard bathroom floor. Here's what you asked for. The woman at the counter suggested these lollipops to help with your morning sickness, so I figured it was worth a try."

"Perfect. I've been looking online to try to find some cute birth announcements. I thought maybe stick with the military theme, but so much of what I'm finding is dealing with pregnancy while he's deployed. But I did find two cute ideas."

Sitting down, I take out my phone and start looking up different ideas as well, while she snacks on the crackers and ginger ale.

"There are a lot of cute ideas that aren't military-related. But they require ordering specialized items."

"I noticed that too. But since we're short on time, we need to find something that we can do. Preferably today."

After we spend about another thirty minutes looking, an idea pops into my head.

"What if we combine a couple of these ideas that we have pulled aside? Then we'll lead him through the house to find you in the sunroom with the big announcement?"

After we put the plans together, I go to the store again to buy what we need. A few special snacks, some small baby shoes, and a chalkboard are on my list. Everything else they already have at home.

Then I text Noah, asking him to take the lunch that I made for Levi to him. When he texts back asking if I'm okay, I say I am and that I'll be done hogging his wife soon.

Once we have everything set up, I go back to Oakside and hunt Noah down.

"I was sent to tell you that Lexi has a surprise for you, and you're supposed to go home now. I'll take over for the rest of the day. When she began to give me the details, I stopped her because I don't need to know that much about how you guys have so much fun." I tried to lead him astray, thinking that it's some bedroom fun that he's heading home for.

Without a minute's hesitation, he goes right out to find Lexi and her surprise. With all that was happening, I'd never gotten to Levi's room, nor had I had a chance to talk to Lexi today. But after all of our fun planning the announcement, I feel a lot better.

When I get to Levi's room, I find him sitting on the couch. He notices me at the door before I even have a chance to knock.

"I was beginning to think I wasn't going to see you today." He pats the sofa next to him.

Walking in, I sit next to him. This is the closest we've been to each other, and again, like a little schoolgirl, I get all giddy inside that I'm able to be so close to him.

"I spent the morning with Lexi at her house. I had something to help her plan," I smile.

"Yeah, what was it?"

"I can't tell you, because you can't know before Noah does. But let's just say that what the two of them have is sickeningly sweet."

Levi doesn't say anything, but his stare is intense as he looks at my face, and his eyes drift from my eyes down to my lips and back. My mouth suddenly feels dry, and I lick my lips, trying to remember if I even put lip gloss on today.

When his eyes land on my lips this time, they stay there. Is it my imagination that he's moving closer, or is it just wishful thinking? I know I should turn away, break the spell, and move on to more safe topics. But even as I'm yelling at myself to do so, my heart is overriding everything and I'm frozen in place.

As he leans even closer, I know this time it's not in my head. Then I feel his breath on my lips a second before he kisses me. His lips are both soft and firm as he takes control of the kiss. I hesitate only a moment before I start kissing him back.

This kiss is one that short circuits my brain, and all my thoughts and worries are quiet for the first time today. His hand cups the back of my head, pulling me closer to him as he deepens the kiss. I rest a hand on his shoulder just to ground myself and remind myself it's real. He is kissing me, and it's not a dream or some figment of my imagination.

As he pulls back, he rests his forehead on mine, and we catch our breath.

Holy shit, Levi kissed me!

# Chapter 8

## Lexi

Mandy did a fabulous job helping me plan this. Also, those lollipops she got for the morning sickness are amazing. After just one, I was feeling a lot better and able to hold down some food.

I'm sitting in the sunroom waiting for Noah to get here. Though I'm a little nervous about telling him, yet at the same time I know he's going to be as happy as I am, if not just a little bit shocked.

Whether we would ever be able to have kids was something I've always known has been in the back of both of our minds. Though we both want kids, we have had many talks about the fact that we'd be completely content if it was just the two of us. Noah has gone above and beyond to make sure that I'm happy all the time, and I knew if all I ever got was him, I would be thrilled.

Finally, I had stopped thinking about getting pregnant and about having kids and didn't even notice that I had missed my period until I woke up sick in the middle of the night last night. Not wanting to wake up Noah, I ran to the guest bathroom.

Thankfully, he bought my excuse that I was just having problems sleeping last night. I used the excuse I couldn't get comfortable because the muscle in my leg kept cramping up, and that's why I was constantly in and out of bed walking it off. Though I felt bad lying to him, once I realized that I could be pregnant, I didn't want to give it away just in case I wasn't.

So today when he said that I could sleep in, and he would be heading to Oakside, I took him up on it. As soon as he was out the door, I pulled out a box of pregnancy tests from under the bathroom sink and took one. When it came back positive, I tried a second one.

That one came up positive as well and then I knew that I wasn't sick, I was pregnant. By the time the sickness had subsided enough for me to start thinking about how to tell Noah, Mandy had shown up.

When I hear the front door close, my nerves start to settle in again.

"Lexi?" Noah calls for me, but I don't respond because I know he'll see the note on the entryway table.

We moved the table in the center of the entryway so there was no way that he could miss it. It's a box of his favorite snack rolls with a note saying, 'if I'm going to get fat then so are you' and then in parentheses, it says to come find me, follow the shoes.

Lining up several shoes, we left a trail leading him from the entryway to where I am in the sunroom. We started with a pair of his combat boots, which we had to dig out from the back of my closet. Then there is a pair of my heels that he loves me wearing when we go out to dinner.

The other shoes are the little baby shoes that Mandy bought while she was out. As I listen to his hesitant footsteps, I know when he's outside the sunroom and he sees the little baby shoes. When his footsteps falter and he stops, I smile.

"Lexi, what's this?"

Still not answering because I want him to walk into the sunroom and see the last part of his surprise. A moment later he appears in the doorway and the first thing he sees is me. I smile and then look over to the chalkboard that we had set up. His eyes follow mine as he reads the message there.

It says, 'Baby Carr reporting for duty, September 2022.' Then, on the bottom of the chalkboard on the ledge rests both of the positive pregnancy tests.

As I watch him read the chalkboard, it's like he can't believe what he's reading. Then he takes a step forward and re-reads it before his eyes land back on me. He's frozen in place, staring at me like he has no idea what to say or do. Then I start to get nervous because maybe he's changed his mind about wanting kids. I take a hesitant step towards him when he looks back at the chalkboard and reads it again.

"Noah?" I ask softly, waiting for his reaction.

This time when he turns to me, I can see the tears in his eyes.

"You're pregnant?" he whispers, and if I wasn't standing so close, I wouldn't have been able to hear him.

When I smile and nod, he starts full-on crying. Then he reaches for me and pulls us both onto the couch. He holds me in his lap and cries into my neck. Turning, I run my hands through his hair and trace the scars on the side of his face.

I have every line of his scars memorized. Every dip, every rise, every contour. Before he had plastic surgery, I had them memorized. Back then, they were a lot nastier than what they are now. And just like it did then, my gentle touch calms him.

When his shoulders stop shaking and he's holding me with his head still buried in my neck, I go back to running my hands through his hair. Then I take a handful of his hair and gently tilt his head so he's looking at me.

As he finally sits up to look at me, he asks, "When did you find out?" One of his hands that were around my waist settles on my stomach in a protective gesture.

"Last night it wasn't my leg bothering me. I was nauseous and sick and didn't want to wake you up. Around three a.m. I realized that my period was also late. I didn't want to get your hopes up, so I waited until you left this morning to take the pregnancy tests. Mandy found me not too long after that. Then she went to the store and got me some stuff to settle my stomach, and together we planned this."

With his other hand, he runs it through my hair and then pulls me in for a kiss. We've been together for over a year now, but every time he kisses me, I still get the butterflies like I did that first time.

When he pulls back from the kiss, he has a huge smile on his face.

"I think we should do something big to tell our families."

"Well, your birthday is coming up. What if I try to get everyone together under the guise of a surprise party for you, but we turn around and surprise them? I think it would be enough of a reason to get your family to come out here."

Since his sisters took over my website, things have been a lot easier financially for his family. Oakside is making more than enough money to pay us both a salary, so he sends his entire military disability check to them every month. It took some reasoning to get them to accept it, but they finally did.

That money has given them a lot of freedom. Already they were able to come out here and see Oakside when it opened. His dad was able to take some time off and go find another job that wasn't so hard on his body. He's now sitting behind a desk and actually making more money than he was at his old job. Plus, it comes with benefits like insurance, a 401K, paid vacation, and the job has many raffles and giveaways for its employees. He won a gift card to a local furniture store, and they were able to redecorate their living room.

His sisters are already planning for college. Lucy got a full scholarship for photography. She had entered a local competition, and there were several schools that her scholarship covered, one of them being in Savannah. After talking with her parents and us, she decided she wanted to go to school in Savannah. To save money on the dorm, food, and other items, she will be staying with us while she goes to school.

In order to have a bit of freedom and quiet time to study, she'll stay in the apartment downstairs. "It'll be good to see them again. We could also get Lucy to decorate the place downstairs and get it ready for her. Also, they could go tour the school as they haven't had a chance to do that yet."

I know his mind's already going a mile a minute, planning everything he wants to do while his parents are here.

Looking over at me, he rubs my stomach again and gives me another soft kiss. Then he gently moves me to sit next to him on the couch.

"Before I take you upstairs and show you just how happy I am about this news, I want to get pictures of how you set this up. It'll be the first photos in the baby book that I plan to start."

Noah stands up and heads back to the front door. That's just like him, wanting to document every moment. Plus, I'm pretty sure our parents once they find out, will want to see those photos and know how I told him.

As soon as he's done with the photos, he swoops me up into his arms and carries me upstairs. After carefully laying me down on the bed, he lies down next to me. Then he pulls up my shirt to expose my belly and starts placing kisses all over it.

"I don't know how you managed to do it, but you always find a new way to make me even happier than I ever thought possible. I love you, Angel, and I can't wait to start this next chapter of our lives together."

The tears flow freely down my face, and I know that I'll have to get used to much more of this over the next nine months.

I've never been happier or looked forward more to getting fat. It's going to be one hell of a ride.

# Chapter 9

## Levi

I can't seem to stop thinking about that kiss. I hadn't meant to kiss her, but the more that I think about it, the happier I am that I did it. One kiss and I'm already addicted to her, so I can't wait to kiss her again, and again, and again.

While I had been struggling with my feelings towards Mandy, that kiss seemed to set everything right. I never had feelings beyond friendship toward her in high school, but spending the last few weeks with her, getting to know her, changed that.

My nurse, Kaitlyn, peeks her head in.

"How are you feeling?"

I know she's referring to the fact that I had PT today. They began the process of fitting me for a prosthetic leg now that I'm a bit more stable. Normally, PT leaves me sore and tired, but today I just feel energized.

"I actually feel pretty good."

She smiles and holds up an envelope for me.

"Your pen pal wrote back." She walks in and sets the letter on the coffee table next to where I'm watching TV.

"Thanks."

"Also, I got a call from Lexi. She's with Mandy, and I was told to tell you that Mandy will be late today. But Noah will be bringing your lunch up."

Kaitlyn winks at me and then walks off. It's no secret with her that Mandy, every day that she works, has been bringing me a homemade lunch.

I pick up the letter from my pen pal and open it up.

*Levi,*

*Yes, I'm that Kade. But my life is a lot simpler now.*

*My wife was left her parents' inn when they died. It's the same one that I stayed at when I originally visited here. Now, I get to help her run it.*

*In Hollywood, everyone knew me. Everywhere I went I was recognized because of the movies that I made. They always wanted something from me, whether it was an autograph, a photo, or to be my best friend for a leg up in the business.*

*Here everyone knows me too. But they know me for me. They know me as Lin's husband, the guy who took the Sunrise Inn to the next level. And they know me as the guy who's always happy to lend a hand if needed.*

*When I get stopped on the streets here, it's mostly people wanting to know how I'm doing, or how my wife and son are doing. Sometimes they stop me to share the latest gossip that's going around town. It's only when the tourists visit do I get stopped and asked for photos and autographs. And I find I don't mind it as much anymore.*

*If you had told me five years ago that this was going to be my life, I would have laughed at you and told you to go F off. My wife's best friend married her high school sweetheart, and that guy has become my best friend. A true friend, something that I hadn't really known the meaning of until I moved here.*

*Though I'm sure you know the meaning of someone who truly has your back with your time in the military, which was something I hadn't had. I hope that you will choose to continue writing me, and I hope that my letters give you a little relief, or a peek into the outside world during your treatment.*

*I've included a photo of my view as I write this letter. The back porch at the inn has amazing ocean views. We're still offseason so there are very few people here and it's mostly just locals on the island. It's one of my favorite times of the year. As we gear up for the season, things become busier and more chaotic.*

*Maybe one day, once you're released from Oakside, you'll come to visit and let the magic of Seaview soothe your soul and charm you. Hope you figure out your next course of action. From what I have read, Oakside and its staff seem to have helped many other people decide the next steps in their lives.*

*My wife wanted me to ask if there is anything that we could send you. Books, puzzles, crafts, music? Her best friend's husband is a big city chef. He was cooking at one of the most popular restaurants in New York City before he came home. She suggested that he could make almost any kind of snack that you like. Just let us know and we'd be happy to send you a care package.*

*Kade*

By the time I'm done reading his letter, I'm smiling ear to ear. Kade has a way of telling a story that makes me forget exactly where I am or why I'm here. The photo he included from the back porch is absolutely stunning. Looking at it, I can see a little bit of grass then my eyes hit the beach and beyond that, there's a beautiful sunset with reds and oranges.

Setting the letter on my desk, I decide to head to the library and use the computer. Now that he has me interested in it, I want to look this place up.

The library here at Oakside is fairly large. It's on the other side of the building from where my room is. As I roll my wheelchair in it's almost like I'm entering a completely different building.

Much of Oakside has been modernized. They've kept a lot of historic details of the building, but here the colors are bright and there are lots of windows and natural light. The room I'm told was the original library and is virtually unchanged. There are two walls on either side with floor-to-ceiling bookcases and the ceiling in this room is easily sixteen feet high, if not more. Where the door leads into the library, that wall also has bookcases framing it. The room is long, and in the center are two rows of desks with computers that patients are free to use.

The far wall has several windows that let in some natural light. In front of the windows are several seating areas to read at or to just relax. The view looks out over the property to where the barn is, and you can even see part of the garden from here.

There are several empty desks, so I take one and pull up the Sunrise Inn. The photos on the website are absolutely beautiful. From the look of it, they operate the place together with the Sunset Inn that is next door and run by Kade's wife's best friend.

They also opened up a bunch of luxury villas that seem to be pretty famous spots for Kade's friends from Hollywood when they come to visit.

The rooms in the pictures look relaxing. Then I check out the town's website, and they have one of those postcard picture perfect main streets right on the water overlooking the harbor. There's a new museum that just opened with some of the town's history that includes pirates as well as other exhibits that look interesting. The island also includes a state park and several other tourist attractions.

When I go back to my room, I'm so lost in thought about what I'm going to say to Kade, I don't notice Lexi and Mandy are waiting in my room with a dog. The dog is a German shepherd and looks like the military police dogs that my unit used to work with.

When the dog sees me, it takes off, running right at me and jumps into my lap. I only get one of the wheels on my wheelchair locked and the force of him jumping into my lap is enough to shake the whole chair. The dog starts licking my face and I'm in shock. After a minute, I start petting him to get him to calm down.

"What's going on?"

Lexi looks over at Mandy, and they exchange a look before Mandy looks back at me.

"About a month ago, your unit was ambushed. Three men died and there were four others who were injured. One of the men who died was Braxton. We recently found out that his dog was up for adoption because the military had discharged him. Unfortunately, the family couldn't take him. So, we decided to bring Ace here to Oakside."

The news hits me like a ton of bricks. We lost two men in the blast that took my leg, and now we've lost three more. Braxton and I didn't know each other before these deployments, but during our time together, we hung out quite a bit. We shared a bunk, and Braxton was assigned to Ace.

Ace and I had bonded. We'd play fetch, and he'd go running with Braxton and me when we'd go in the mornings or in the evenings when we were trying to tire ourselves out for bed.

I looked down at Ace who's now sitting in my lap, and realize that he's lost an eye. On the same side where he's injured his eye, there are some patches where there's no fur.

"What happened to Ace here?"

"There was an explosion, and he tried to save Braxton. When he couldn't, he went in and dragged one of the other men who did survive to safety. In doing so, he lost his eye and had some burns along the side of his body. Of course, the military treated him and covered all of his vet bills, but then they discharged him," Lexi says.

Continuing to pet Ace, I look down at him and he looks back at me and in his eye there's sadness. Honestly, I swear I can detect relief that he finally sees a familiar face. I rest my forehead on his, and let out a few tears for a fallen brother, and for my friends. When I lift my head again, Ace rests his head on my shoulder and just sits there not only giving some comfort, but soaking it up from me.

I look up at Lexi and Mandy to find them both staring at me, and watching how Ace is interacting with me.

"Can he stay with me? He's been through a lot. Maybe seeing a familiar face right now will do him some good."

"Did you work with him?" Mandy asks.

"Braxton was my bunkmate when we were deployed. I hadn't met him before that deployment, but after we hung out and got to know each other. Ace here would come running with us in the morning or in the evening. He was always around when we're playing cards and had downtime. Braxton and I were assigned to many of the same duties, so we interacted and Ace was right there. When Braxton would take the time to take a shower, Ace liked to sit with me or play fetch with me."

"You and Ace we're pretty close?" Lexi asks

"Yeah, we were. Had I known he was up for adoption, I would have done everything I could to adopt him myself, even though I'm still here."

"Many of the patients here have benefited from working with therapy dogs or even having a service dog of their own," Lexi says. "You are no different. Ace is more than welcome to stay with you. Just make sure you ask the nurse for help if you need to take him outside. I'll have some dishes, food, and a dog bed brought for him." Lexi tells me, a small smile on her face.

Ace starts shifting around in my lap. He's a full-grown German shepherd and a pretty big dog who's definitely having trouble fitting in my wheelchair.

"What do you say, Ace? You want to stay here with me?"

Ace barks and then pants a little bit, which causes both of the girls to laugh.

"I'm going to go get the stuff for Ace and I'll be back," Mandy says before they both leave, closing the door behind them.

When the door shuts, Ace jumps off my lap and starts sniffing around. Then I go to my desk and pull out a piece of paper to write Kade back. I'm going to take him up on his offer of a care package, only I plan on telling him all about Ace, and asking for a doggie care package instead.

# Chapter 10

## Mandy

Today I am spending the morning at Lexi's house with her and Paisley. Since she's been dealing with morning sickness, she hasn't been getting into Oakside until the afternoons when she's feeling a bit better, so we decided to have our weekly meeting here.

Paisley and I are still the only ones who know she is pregnant. We have been sworn to secrecy because we are helping plan the party for Noah's surprise birthday that will surprise everyone. Noah's parents already have their tickets and plan to visit. Also, we have a few people from Oakside that will be attending along with Lexi's family.

As Paisley and I walk over together, we go over party ideas, and let ourselves in per Lexi's instructions.

"The house is really quiet. Do you think maybe she's still sleeping?" Paisley asks.

"Last time, I found her upstairs in her bathroom. Let's go check there." Paisley follows me upstairs, and sure enough, Lexi is sitting pretty much in the same spot on her bathroom floor as I found her last time.

She groans when she sees us. "I really thought I'd at least be downstairs by the time you guys got here."

Seeing her misery, I grab a clean washcloth from the shelf and run it under some cool water, wring it out and then place it on her forehead.

"Are the lollypops not working anymore?" I ask because I know that they were helping her earlier this week.

"I don't know," she wails. "Noah bought me some more, but they're downstairs on the kitchen counter, and I haven't been able to get down there."

She barely has time to finish her sentence before she's leaning over the toilet again. At this point, she's just dry heaving because she doesn't have anything left to throw up.

As I rub her back, I say to Paisley. "Why don't you go see if you can find the lollipops in the kitchen?" She nods, jumping up, and is out of the room before I can even say another word.

"Talk to me about work. Something, anything to take my mind off of this, please," Lexi says as Paisley walks back into the room with the lollipops.

"Here's something that should take your mind off of it. Levi kissed me." I say with a huge smile on my face.

Paisley starts giggling, and Lexi even manages a smile.

"When? We need more details than that," Paisley says.

"Well, it happened last week the same day that you found out that you were pregnant," I say, looking at Lexi.

We spend the next several minutes talking about Levi. They want more details on how I know him, and what he was like in school. Since Lexi knows some of the story, she's the one to ask the big question.

"So, your friend Rebecca is cool with all this?" Lexi asks, leaning back against the bathroom cabinet.

"Honestly, that's what I was coming to talk to you about the day that you found out you were pregnant. But we got sidetracked for the best possible reason. I haven't talked to Rebecca about it. In fact, I haven't even told her Levi's here, and part of me doesn't want to because I know she's going to show up and feel this obligation to be there for him."

"Wouldn't that be a good thing to have someone else to help him out while he's recovering?" Paisley asks.

I'm hesitant to answer because my answer doesn't even make sense to me. But I figure if I at least get it out there, maybe they can help me sort through my feelings. If anyone can, it'll be one of these two girls.

"In theory, yes. But in my gut, I feel like the moment she steps back into the picture, then it's over for Levi and me, and I really want to see where this goes."

"Then you really need to talk to her. Get it out in the open, and then you'll know what to do. But in all honesty, Levi has a choice in this too. If Rebecca becomes overwhelming, he can limit the amount of time she's able to visit him. At any point, we will happily enforce new rules for any patient," Lexi says.

"Yep, I know that one all too well," Paisley says.

I remember when Paisley's brother found out about her and Easton. He wasn't too happy, and it caused a rift between Paisley and Easton. That's when Easton stopped allowing

Paisley to visit, and Lexi and Noah had to enforce it.

"Okay, I'll talk to her. Actually, she's in Savannah right now. We have plans to meet up the day after tomorrow on my day off and spend the day together and do lunch. I guess that's a perfect time to tell her. Now, let's get back to the main reason we're here. Let's talk about plans for the Aquatic Center."

With all the publicity that we've gotten, it has brought in a good number of donations. Enough to at least start making plans for the Aquatic Center. There's so much to consider. We need to get the plans drawn up, talk with professionals on what needs to be done, and maybe even clear the land where we would like to have it located.

"I'll message Judy and Keith, who run the rehabilitation home in Texas, and see who they recommend. They have a beautiful Aquatic Center." Lexi says as she finishes the lollipop that she's been sucking on.

"So, the easy part with the barn is set up," I say. "We have a barn manager and a few ranch hands, but we still need an equine therapist to help. With your permission, I'll go ahead and put out a job posting and let the staff know that we're looking to see if they might know someone. I'm assuming, like all the other people that work here, we want them to have some kind of military affiliation?"

It's not exactly a requirement that people must have a military connection to work here, but we do like for the therapists and doctors to at least have worked with the military or have an association to understand the men and women here better here.

"Yes, on the connection, and yes, go ahead and post it."

We go over a few more small things on budgets and a few changes that have been submitted by the staff. Lexi tells us a local bookstore dropped off several large boxes of books for us to stock our library with, and we then we discuss some other new donations that we received.

By the time we finish up with the meeting, we're able to get Lexi fed and feeling a lot better, and she comes back over to Oakside with us just in time for lunch.

"I'm going to go find Noah now," Lexi tells me. "I know you have lunch to take to Levi, so go and have your lunch date."

She smiles at me before leaving to find her husband.

Going to my office, I get our lunch from the mini-fridge I have in there. Last weekend I made a large pot roast, so we're having leftovers today. Then I go upstairs to the nurse's room and warm up the food, arranging it on plates before adding it to a tray and taking it to Levi's room.

When I get there, he's already sitting on the couch and smiling, so I set the tray down and hand him his plate.

"Pot roast was always my favorite meal that my mom would make. She prepared it on Sundays, and it was a required meal that everyone had to be home for no matter what, and that meant including my father." Levi says as he digs into the food. After his first bite, he's groaning and shoveling it in like someone is threatening to take the plate away.

"Slow down, soldier. This isn't the mess hall, and you aren't being timed on how fast you can eat." I chuckle, taking my first bite as he's already halfway done with his food.

Taking a sip of water, he smiles at me and says, "Old habits die hard."

I keep thinking about the conversation that I had this morning with the girls and decide that I need to tell him that I'm at least going to see Rebecca and see what he says.

"So, my next day off, I'm heading down to Savannah."

"Shopping trip?" he smiles.

"Kind of. Rebecca's husband has some meetings in Savannah, and she tagged along. We're going to meet up and have lunch." I say, with some apprehension.

When he looks up at me again, he looks slightly hesitant. Rebecca has been the big elephant in the room that we haven't really talked about. I think neither of us is willing to broach that subject because we both know that we should have talked to her before anything ever started between us. Not that any of this was planned.

"I think I need to talk to her about us," I say very slowly, not really wanting to say the words but knowing that I need to.

"I agree. But just so you know, no matter what she says, it doesn't change how I feel about you. I'm in this, and someone's outside opinion isn't going to sway me."

"Well, it's a little more difficult for me. Rebecca's been my best friend for so long. I value her friendship because I didn't have a lot of people that I could rely on in my life."

He looks at me with understanding in his eyes instead of judgment and squeezes my hand in reassurance.

"You tell her whatever you're comfortable with. Then we'll get to the rest together. I'm not going anywhere, literally." He jokes, saying the last part with a half-smile, but I know he means he'll have my back.

We continue eating our lunch, discussing safe topics like the new books that were just donated. As we finish up, Ace appears next to Levi.

"I forgot that he was here. He's been so good. Most dogs will bark at your feet until you feed them something." I say, scratching behind Ace's ear.

"He was trained not to beg, but he always gets something when I'm finished eating." Levi gives him a piece of pot roast off his fork and then lets Ace lick the plate. When he sets the plate on the coffee table, Ace lays down at his feet, calm and relaxed, like I wish I was right now.

Levi wraps his arm around my shoulder and pulls me to his side. I rest my head on his shoulder and relax into him. He turns on the TV to some funny sitcom, and as he holds me, the stress of the situation just melts away.

"Thank you. I guess I needed this more than I realized." I lean up to give him a kiss on the cheek, but he turns his head and captures my mouth with his. The kiss is tentative, almost as if he expects me to pull back or to stop him.

When I keep my lips planted on his, he turns his body into mine and deepens the kiss. Wanting him closer, I wrap my arms around his waist and hold on to him. This kiss feels different from the others, more important. Without words he's showing me how he feels and that he meant what he said, no matter what happens with Rebecca. He's not going anywhere.

I try to let go of all my insecurities of losing one of the few people who have always been there for me, and try to be in the moment, be here with him. Then I feel the stress leave me in waves, and it's replaced with the feeling of being so damn turned on I can barely stand it.

This kiss is slow, simmering, and we get lost in it. His hand skims over my breast, and I gasp with the pleasure of it. It feels so good, too good. Then his tongue creates a whirlwind of sensations in me before he gently pulls away, groaning.

"It's so easy to get lost in you." He says, placing a soft kiss on my lips before retreating back to his side of the couch.

It is way too easy to get lost in him, too, and I know that will be our downfall.

# Chapter 11

## Mandy

Today, I'm heading down to Savannah to meet up with Rebecca. I should be excited to visit my best friend, go shopping, and have lunch. I should be thrilled to gush over her being pregnant, but all I feel is dread.

I dread having to tell my best friend about Levi. I dread her reaction, and most of all, I dread mine if our little bubble is popped. No matter what, I know from today on, things will never be the same. What I don't know is, if it's going to be a good thing or a bad thing.

The closer I get to Savannah, the more I attempt to take my mind off that conversation. Though I watch the signs and try to take in my surroundings, it doesn't work. We're meeting at the visitor center because she wants to do one of the historic trolley tours before we stop and have lunch. So, I drive straight to the park.

After taking a few deep breaths, I collect my thoughts before I go inside to meet Rebecca. Stepping into the welcome center, it's a flurry of activity, even for a weekday, but she spots me before I even get a chance to get my bearings.

"Mandy!" she calls from my left as she rushes over to me.

Her blonde curls bounce over her shoulders, and a huge smile lights up her face. She's wearing a maxi dress and high heels. You'd never know she was pregnant if it weren't for the baby bump that's starting to show.

She wraps me into a hug that is a little awkward with the baby bump between us.

"So, Dale dropped me off early, and I went around and looked at each of the different tours and picked the one that I think we should do." She thrusts a brochure into my hands.

"Well, I trust your opinion. When does the tour leave?"

"In ten minutes. Come on." She grabs my hand and pulls me out to the parking lot, where the different open-air trolleys are lined up. Each trolley is a different color, and while they seem to boast pretty much the same tour, I guess there are different stops around town.

We buy our tickets and take our seats. I let her have the window, I figure with the news I have to tell her today it's the least I can do.

"I chose this one because it's a ninety-minute history tour all around downtown Savannah and has all the best stops. Then we can get on and off all day as we move around downtown. It'll save my feet just a little." She says excitedly with her ever-present bubbly personality.

"And you even wore high heels." I joke with her.

She opens her purse and pulls out a pair of what looks like socks.

"Of course, I have my purse flats, so as soon as my feet hurt, I can put these babies on, and I'm good to go. Then I can slip my heels back on before I see Dale again, and he'll never know."

"You know you're pregnant, right? It's all right not to be able to wear high heels still all day."

She waves me off as the tour starts. We both have our phones out, taking photos at different places that we stop. Once we see all the famous downtown buildings and all the different parks, as well as hearing some of the legends, we decide our list of things we'd love to see and do gets too long for just one day. Then Rebecca starts talking about coming back and spending a weekend for a girls' trip after the baby is born.

All I want is to get everything concerning Levi off my chest. If I can get it over with and be honest with her, I'd be happy. But I think in the middle of a trolley where she can't storm off doesn't seem like the best choice.

Cutting into my thoughts, Rebecca says, "So, I think if we get off at this stop it'll be the shortest walk to the restaurant that I've been really wanting to try for lunch." Then she holds open the map showing me the different trolley stops as we near the end of the tour. I agree with her, as I'm not going to argue about where to eat, not today.

When we get off the trolley, she links her arm through mine as we walk down the sidewalk toward this restaurant that promises all the high-calorie southern foods that you can eat. The stuff that she wouldn't dare touch if she wasn't pregnant.

"One thing they don't warn you about when you're      pregnant      are      the      pregnancy nightmares." She says as we walk a bit slower to lunch.

"What do you mean?" I ask.

"They are so vivid, you can touch and smell things, and you wake and it feels so real like you're not dreaming. When I had a dream Dale was cheating on me, I thought for a whole week he was!"

"Dale loves you, like crazy in love with you; he wouldn't cheat," I tell her, and I mean it.

"I know that, and that's what confused me so much. I followed him to work for a week. He found it amusing, but I couldn't shake the feelings or emotions."

"Why did you follow him to work?"

"Because in the dream, he was cheating with his secretary."

I burst out laughing. Dale's secretary is a few years away from retirement. She's in her fifties and is as excited about their baby as a grandma would be.

"It's not funny!!"

"Did you tell him about this?"

"Yes, and his secretary even understood. When she had her youngest, she had them really bad. She kept dreaming someone was kidnapping her kids, and even holding her kids in her arms didn't calm her."

"What did Dale say when you told him?"

"Oh, Mandy, I don't deserve him. He took me up to a little lounge area in his office and said I could come to work with him every day. He even offered to put a playpen in for the baby." Tears start falling, and she wipes them away and laughs at herself, changing the subject.

She begins telling me about what meetings Dale is at today. Mentally shaking my head, I focus on Rebecca as we enter the small little restaurant that's taken over an old historic home.

"What's on your mind? You seem to be a million miles away right now," she asks after we order our drinks and lunch.

"Let me ask you something," I say, chickening out a bit.

"You can ask me anything. You should know that by now, Mandy," she says in a very serious tone.

That's one thing about Rebecca. She can be bubbly and energetic and can total rock the dumb blonde routine, but she's crazy smart and knows when to be serious. If it weren't for this side of her, we wouldn't have stayed friends for so long.

"How would you feel if I were dating one of your ex-boyfriends?" I ask, broaching the topic.

Taking a sip of her sweet tea, she gives it some serious thought. Before answering, she studies me closely.

"I guess it would depend on which one. If it was a guy that I had slept with, I don't think I'd be okay with it. But then again, I have Dale, and I really have no feelings toward any of my exes anymore, and if it made you happy, I guess I could deal with it. Why are you asking?"

When the waitress sets down our food, it gives me time to think of my response. I feel like I need more answers from her before I can spill everything about Levi and me.

"So, if it had been someone that you had slept with and I said that I had started talking to him and maybe we had been out on a few dates, maybe he's even kissed me, how would you react to that?"

She laughs, taking a bite of her fried chicken.

"Back in our college days, I would have said that would be breaking the girl code and I would have been furious. Now? Again, I guess it would depend on who it is. If it were any of the frat boys I dated in college I really wouldn't care. If it was Levi I'd probably be pretty upset, but I know you wouldn't do that to me because you're my friend. Why are you asking?"

Without a doubt, I know I need to come clean, and I know I need to tell her. I should tell her now and be honest and open. I deserve her anger. Also, I know if I tell her now, we can work it out. While I know all this and I'm trying to figure out the words to say, the next thing I know, I hear myself lying to my best friend, and I'm not even sure I consciously did it.

"One of my friends at work is in a situation like that, and I'm not quite sure how to help her. It's been on my mind because she's been torn up about telling her friend about it."

Rebecca nods her head, looking serious for a moment. I must be holding my breath, thinking that she's going to call me out on it. She *should* call me out on it.

"I guess if she hasn't told her friend about it, she should do it now before it gets any more serious. If they've only started talking, it's not that big of a deal because it might not go anywhere. But if they've moved on and they've even shared a kiss, then she really needs to be honest and open if she wants to keep that friendship."

It's just like Rebecca that she would take it seriously even though she doesn't know the supposed other girl, and she would give me advice to help someone else out. But the back of my brain is screaming that she's giving you another out. Tell her the truth, tell her now, and just beg for her forgiveness.

The thoughts go around in my head, and I open my mouth several times, but I can't seem to get any words out. The fear of possibly losing her friendship paralyzes me, and I wait too long to say anything. She takes my silence as the end of the conversation and switches topics.

I missed my window, and I'm not sure that I'm upset that I did.

# Chapter 12

## Levi

Today is the big day, my prosthetic leg is here. They're going to show me how to put it on and take it off, and then I'm going to do some PT with it on. The doctors have gone over and over everything with me so many times I can recite it by heart.

I'm not going to be able to walk overnight. According to them, I'm going to be very unsteady, which means I need to continue with my PT, but if I keep it up eventually, I won't even notice it's there. I always laugh when they say that last part because there's a huge difference between your own leg and a metal leg.

Though I guess I'm lucky enough that if I wear long pants and the right shoes, no one will ever know that the leg is not mine when I'm out and about. But I will know, I will always know. Those that are close to me will know. Mandy will know.

Ace is picking up on my anxiety before this appointment, and he hasn't left my side. Even when I took him to the courtyard to do his business, he took one step away from my wheelchair, peed in a flowerpot, and then was ready to come back inside. I will say it is nice not to have to go through this alone. Having Ace by my side has been an unexpected, but welcome help.

Part of me wants Mandy at my appointment. Not only do I want her support, but I want to at least hold her hand. But the larger part of me doesn't want her to see me like that, to see where my leg used to be and everything that I'm missing. She's never once made me feel uncomfortable about it, but again I've been able to hide it pretty well with long pants and blankets on my lap.

There's a knock on the door, and I turn my head to find nurse Kaitlyn poking her head in.

"All right, I'm taking you down to PT myself because I'm not letting you out of this appointment," she says with a big smile lighting up her face. She's been my biggest cheerleader even when I didn't want people around me.

"I figured there was no getting out of it. Ace has been looking forward to this appointment for a while. I wouldn't want to disappoint him." I grumble but allow her to maneuver my wheelchair out into the hallway.

"Now I know they told you that you'll probably be sore for the first few days. So you make sure you let me know if you need anything for the pain or if you need any rub for your leg," she says as we enter the lobby.

I nod in agreement, but can't say anything because Mandy is there in the lobby, and she looks like she's been waiting on me.

"I know we don't normally do the whole before an appointment thing, but today is a really big day, and I would really like to take you to your appointment if you're okay with that," Mandy says. Her look is hesitant like she doesn't want to overstep, and I really appreciate that.

Looking back at nurse Kaitlyn, I nod, "It's fine. I think I'd like her to take me."

"I'll check in after your appointment," she says, giving my shoulder a squeeze before she turns and goes down the hallway we just came from. Mandy walks over and pats Ace on the head before taking my hand and giving it a squeeze. Then she takes Kaitlyn's spot behind me to push the wheelchair.

Once we enter the hallway that will take us down to the PT room, Mandy finally speaks.

"When we first opened, we had another man who lost his leg. The day that he went to get his prosthetic, he says he had never been so nervous in his life. I know it's scary. It's the unknown and is the start of a completely different life, and I get that. I also want you to know that I'm here for you, to help in any way that you need or want. But it's okay not to want my help either."

Between the door for the library and the door for the PT room, there is a bench, and she sits down on it facing me, pulling scooting close so that her knee is touching my knee on my good leg.

She takes my hand in hers and smiles at me, rubbing her thumb over the back of my hand.

"Remember, it's okay not to be okay," She repeats the words she said to me many weeks ago.

"To be honest, I don't know what I'm feeling right now."

"And that's fine. At least you're being honest about it." She sits with me for a few more minutes, neither of us really saying anything before she leans forward carefully avoiding my bad leg, and her lips land on mine.

It's a soft, sweet kiss, nothing like the kisses we have shared in my room, but it is our first public kiss, not that anyone is here to see it. Though she pulls away way too soon, I take a moment and stare at her.

We still haven't talked about her visit with Rebecca yesterday. She hasn't been overly thrilled to talk about the trip to Savannah in general, and in all honesty, I'm scared to ask, so I focused on today's appointment. But I guess it's a conversation that we can have later.

Breaking the silence, Mandy asks, "So, there's this little place in town that makes handmade ice cream, and I was thinking of making a run and going and getting us some ice cream to celebrate this appointment. Do you want me to meet you in your room, or would you rather have some space?"

"Space is the last thing I want. Mint chocolate chip ice cream is my favorite, and we both know we have more than one thing to talk about later." I hint about her trip yesterday. If I can make it through this appointment, I'm not going to let her dance around the subject anymore.

"Deal. It's not that I didn't want to tell you; it's that I didn't want to tell you before your appointment."

That's when my physical therapist peeks his head out the door and tells me that he's ready for me.

"Come here." I motion for her, and when she's close, I pull her in for another kiss. "I meant it. I'm not going anywhere."

"Neither am I. Now go give him hell."

Vince, my physical therapist, smiles and closes the door behind me. Beginning my appointment like all the others, he asks me the usual questions. How am I doing, how am I feeling, and has anything changed? Then I get fitted for my leg.

They have me sitting in what I call one of the waiting rooms. The chairs are very basic and uncomfortable. In the room are my doctor, my physical therapist, my therapist, Noah, and Easton. Noah told me he and Easton would be there today because no one goes through this alone. That means more to me than he realizes.

Before anything else happens, there are some whispers, and then a man steps out of Vince's office. At first, I don't recognize him until he comes closer. This is Kade. The man I've been writing.

"Kade here wanted to be here and support you today," Noah says.

"I know this is going to be hard and emotional, and if you don't want me here, there are no hard feelings," Kade says.

"Stay. I'm really glad you are. Maybe we can do lunch before you leave?" I suggest, and a smile fills his face.

"I'd like that. Tomorrow, if you are up for it?"

"What Kade isn't saying is that he also made a few upgrades to your prosthetic," Vince says.

"What?" I ask, confused.

"My wife started doing some research and talked my ear off. The military would give you a perfectly fine one that would be everything you need. But we decided that wasn't good enough," he shrugs.

That's when Vince brings the box over, and sets it on the table in front of me, and opens it. I have been expecting a very basic prosthetic with a place for my stump and the ability to bend my knee. But what sits in the box in front of me is the Ferrari of prosthetics.

Kade is excited as he tells me, "There is a cooling gel bag, so you don't have any friction rubbing your skin while it's on. It's super light, waterproof so you can go swimming or wear it in the shower. You can leave the metal exposed like this, or there are some sleeves to cover it up, and it will look just like you are wearing a brace or tight athletic pants. Lin says there are a bunch of designs you can get too." Kade's smile gets bigger and bigger.

"You can walk, run or jog in it, it's great for driving, and you will be able to sit on the ground and get up again without anyone knowing you have a prosthetic once you master PT," Vince adds.

I can easily read between the lines. Kade paid for this. This man who hadn't met me before today, who only knew a little about me via letters, gave me this amazing gift.

"I can't even tell you what this means to me," I say as I order my eyes to stop watering.

The specialist they brought in who's been working with me comes in and kneels on the floor in front of me. My heart is racing so hard I'm afraid it'll beat out of my chest. For a minute, I wish Mandy was here because she always knows how to calm me. But in the next moment, when he lifts my pant leg and exposes the stub that's left of my leg, I'm glad she's not here.

He starts showing me how to attach the prosthetic and explaining all sorts of details. Noah places his hand on my shoulder, and when he goes to remove it, I cover his hand with mine. Right now, that little bit of contact is something I need desperately. He doesn't move, and I swear it seems like everyone in the room is holding their breath.

"All right. Why don't you stand up and see how it feels? It's going to take a lot of getting used to." The specialist says as he stands up and moves to the side.

When I look at the device that's now on my leg and put my pant leg over it, you'd never be able to tell the difference. It's designed to be able to put on whatever pair of shoes that I'm wearing. They had already put on the other sneaker I had brought with me.

That's when Ace walks over and starts sniffing around me. He wants to know what the other guy did and make sure everything is okay. I lift my pant leg to show him the prosthetic, and he sniffs it out for a minute and then rests his head on my good leg.

Then I give his head a good scratch, but he doesn't move, and, at that moment, I know there's one person missing. So, I turn to Noah, and he seems to know what I'm going to ask before even saying it.

"Can you, um... ask... Mandy, to join us?" He's already on his phone calling her.

A moment later, she comes rushing in with her phone in hand.

"What's wrong? Is he okay?" She's a little frantic. When I look at Noah, he's smirking.

"I don't even want to know what you said to her," I say as people part, and she stands by my side. I hold my hand out to her, and she takes it without hesitation.

"They just put the prosthetic on, and he's getting ready to stand up for the first time. He wanted you here," Noah says the words I can't seem to get out of my mouth.

Looking up at Mandy, her eyes seem a little misty, but she smiles at me and squeezes my hand.

"Alright, are you ready?" Vince asks, and I give a sharp nod and reluctantly let go of Mandy's hand.

Vince steps in front of me and places my arms on his to steady myself. Then I stand up for the first time in months. Once I'm steady, he slowly backs away, and I'm standing on my own. No bar to hang onto and no one with their arm around my waist for me to keep me upright, just me on my own two feet even if one of those feet isn't the one I was born with.

Once I'm in this prosthetic, there's a shift inside of me. Before, I was so angry, and all of a sudden, I'm so grateful. Mandy slowly moves to stand in front of me, and the tears that were glistening in her eyes are now freely flowing down her cheeks.

"I am so damn proud of you," she whispers before she tenderly places her hands on either side of my face and leans in to kiss me. I place both of my hands on her waist and gently hold her to me and, for the first time, feel her pressed completely against me.

There are little things I didn't realize that I was missing. But this moment, when I'm able to feel her completely against me as she kisses me, and simply being able to stand on my own is one I'll never forget.

When she pulls back, I carefully wipe some of the tears from her face, and she runs her hands gently through my hair. Suddenly everyone in the room starts clapping, and just like that, the bubble that's just been the two of us bursts. Her cheeks flame bright red, and it's the sexiest thing I have ever seen. If I were a bit steadier, I'd pull her into me and let her bury her face in my neck. But holding her hands right now is the best I can offer her.

"Thank you so much for being here, but I think that as they make all these adjustments that I'll be alright." My girl is bright and can read between the lines.

She gently leans in and gives me a kiss on the cheek.

"I'm going to go get that ice cream, and I'll be waiting in your room when you're done," she says with a wobbly smile on her face.

I can only nod because emotions are clogging my throat, and I don't want her to know. She leans down and pets Ace, who eats up the attention.

"You take good care of him, and I'll even bring you back a little snack." Ace gives a single bark like he knows exactly what she's saying, and everyone laughs as she leaves. She pauses and looks at Kade but doesn't say anything as she leaves.

The next hour is a flurry of activity, making any final adjustments on the leg and showing me how to take it on and off. Well, I should say, forcing me to take it on and off so that I could prove I understand how to do it.

Vince takes me through some basic movements and tells me that I should be wearing the prosthetic while I'm sitting down and let myself get used to it. But until he gives me the okay, I'm not to be walking around on it. Though now, I'm to wear it to every one of my appointments.

By the time I make it back to my room, I'm exhausted, but seeing Mandy waiting there for me gives me a second wind. When I wheel over to the couch, she leans in to give me a kiss.

"I'm going to go get the ice cream from the freezer, and I'll be right back." She's up and out the door as I maneuver myself to the couch before she gets back.

As she sits down, she's holding three cups of ice cream, and she hands me mine, but I look over at the other two in her hands.

"Why do you have three cups?" I ask her.

She holds up one cup that has a bunch of sprinkles on it. "This one it's mine. It's a birthday cake ice cream, frosting and all. But this one is for Ace. They called it a pup ice cream cup."

When she hands me Ace's, I smile. I love that she thought of him. Taking the cup from her, I remove the lid and set it on the floor for him. Where most dogs would attack the ice cream cup like someone might take it away at any moment, Ace lays down, places a leg on either side of the cup, and takes his time eating it.

"I don't think I've ever seen a dog so well behaved." Mandy laughs as she takes her first bite of ice cream.

"Now, let's address the elephant in the room so that I can just hold you and watch some TV. It's been a long day already." I level her with a glance as I take a bite of my ice cream.

Closing my eyes for just a moment, I enjoy this ice cream. Not only is it really good, but the perfect little treat after my PT session today.

Mandy is looking down at her lap instead of making eye contact with me, so I have the feeling it didn't go very well. Reaching out, I take her hand, giving her reassurance.

"I kind of chickened out, but not really in a way," she says.

I have no freaking clue what that means, and I still can't see her face to try to read anything from it.

"And what exactly does that mean?"

"Well, when we got down to Savannah, we did one of the trolley rides, and we talked, and it was just so good to be around her. I guess I missed her more than I realized. After the trolley ride, we went and had lunch, and I just wanted to test the waters, so I presented our situation to her as if one of the girls at Oakside was having this issue instead of me."

"And what exactly did she say?"

"In short, that she wouldn't be okay with it. Part of me wonders if she knew that I wasn't talking about someone else because she did give me an out to tell her, and I completely chickened out. I'm so sorry, especially after watching how brave you were today when I couldn't even form words to tell someone something yesterday. I can't even imagine what you think of me right now." She's still looking down at her lap, and that's when I start to see the tears fall.

Setting my ice cream down on the coffee table, I pull her over into my arms, and she buries her head into my neck. Then I take her ice cream and set it on the coffee table too.

"I was able to do everything today because I had you by my side. If you weren't in that room today, I don't know if I would have been brave enough to stand up. So having to stand in front of your best friend and tell her something she might not like had to have been scary as hell. Maybe this is something that we have to do together, and if that's the case, I'm more than willing to stand by your side when we do it."

That just seems to make her cry a bit harder, and I hold her tightly in my arms through the storm. My head understands how scared she must have been and how complicated the situation is.

But my heart is wondering if this means that she'll choose Rebecca over me.

# Chapter 13

## Mandy

Today I am giving tours around Oakside to a few very rich friends of one of our former patients. Since Teddy has been released from Oakside and gotten on his feet again, he has been an incredible asset for paying it forward to the soldiers still here.

He is also friends with Owen, who is the husband of one of Lexi's good friends. Also a billionaire, Owen has been extremely generous in helping Oakside out. Also, he assisted in lining up a few of these men that I'm giving a tour to today as well.

When Owen decided to sponsor a soldier who needed help but was having issues with his insurance, I had the idea of starting an Adopt A Soldier program.

Lexi told me to run with the idea, so I set up a program where we would have people on call who were open to sponsoring soldiers whose insurance didn't cover any or all of their treatment. Then they would pay the monthly fee for the soldier to be here for the length of the soldier's treatment. If they weren't currently sponsoring a soldier, they wouldn't be sending a monthly donation unless they wanted to.

Of course, Owen and Teddy were the first two to sign up for the program and one of Owen's friends signed up without even seeing Oakside. So these men I'm bringing around aren't just looking to donate. These men are interested in the Adopt A Soldier program. But before throwing money at the program, these men wanted to tour the grounds and actually get to be more hands-on and involved.

I have to give them credit. They didn't come flashing their money around. If you had no idea who they were, you would never know that they have money with the way they're dressed so casually in jeans and shirts. Well, other than the fancy cars they showed up in.

Right now, we're down in my office, and I just went over all the details of the new program and let them ask any questions they had upfront. When Noah knocks on my office door, I'm about to go show them around upstairs.

He had agreed to stop by and share his story about how he and Lexi had started Oakside. Since Lexi is still fighting morning sickness, she's not here otherwise, she would be right by his side.

"Gentlemen, this is Noah. He is one of the founders of Oakside and was the first unofficial patient as well. He and his wife have put their blood, sweat, and tears into building this place and getting it up and running. I invited him to help with the tour, but even more so to share his story."

Noah takes a few minutes and tells the story of how his unit was hit by an IED, and he sustained substantial burns. He tells them about when he was at the hospital in Germany how he met Lexi, who was the sister of his unit leader. After talking about the surgeries he had to endure, he even shares a few before and after photos of himself.

Continuing, he says how this house was Lexi's, and when he was able to leave and didn't have any place to go except the rehabilitation wing at the hospital, Lexi couldn't let that happen. Instead, she brought him home and made a very rough makeshift version for him of what Oakside is today.

In closing, he talks about how that started the dream and possibilities for Oakside to help other soldiers. Then seeing Easton in the hospital and wanting to help him, he knew Oakside would provide a place for Easton to heal. Then he wraps up by explaining how Easton was one of the first five patients and is now head of security here.

I've heard this story so many times, and every time I still get goosebumps. I don't know how you could hear his story and not. It's so heart-wrenching. Then again, almost every guy here has a heart-wrenching story to share. Whether they share it or not is left up to them.

After that, I give them a tour of the downstairs. It includes the kitchen facility, the offices, and our staff rooms.

Once upstairs, we take them right to the lobby, and of course, there are lots of oohs and aahs about how we kept so much of the historical value of the house.

"What kind of history does this place have?" Randy asks.

It turns out that Randy is a Texas oil tycoon. Owen says he's new money and is looking for ways to give back because he didn't have a lot growing up. He seems pretty down to earth from the few conversations we've had.

"It was an old southern plantation that had tobacco and cotton plants on most of the land. That was part of the over seven-hundred-acre plantation that has been sold off. We now have roughly eighty acres of it attached to Oakside. During the Civil War, when the Union troops traveled through, there was a fire here, and it caused an uprising with the slaves on the property. So, the back part of this house has had some reconstruction after the war, but the front part of the house is completely original to the day it was built." I tell them.

"Out to the back of the property, there are some of the original slave quarter homes. They were damaged in the fire as well, and a few of them are only the foundation. Because they are on the National Historical database, we can't do anything about them, and that's about one-half of an acre of the property. But we have made a walking trail out there, and many of the residents like to use it as part of their daily regiment to take a stroll out that way to see the ruins," Noah says.

We make the rounds, and they meet a few patients, see some of the rooms, and even run into Easton and his dog Allie, which they get a kick out of. We show them the garden outside and the newly restored barn, and then Noah takes them over to his house for lunch and to meet with Lexi.

At the end of the tour, I visit Levi and collapse on his couch. It's just after lunch, and I'm already exhausted. There had been some pretty late nights putting together this Adopt A Soldier plan.

"So, how did it go?" Levi asks.

"I think it went well. Some of the men are more interested in the history of the building than what we actually do here. But if they donate because they want to help preserve the building, then I'll take it. I really don't care why they donate, just that they donate."

My phone dings letting me know that I have an email, correction, that I have a work email. I checked my phone and sit straight up when I see the email that Noah had attached.

"Holy shit!"

I stare at my email, unable to believe what I'm looking at.

"Everything okay? What's wrong?" Levi asks as he wheels himself over to the couch, as close to me as he can get.

"Noah took the guys over to lunch at his house, and he just sent me five signed contracts for the Adopt A Soldier program. On top of that, each one has donated to Oakside above and beyond what we asked."

"That's a good thing, right?"

"That's a very good thing. I'm in shock. It also means I'm going to be working late tonight because Noah wants to get this donation money budgeted as soon as possible. Between the five of them, they just donated a million dollars, plus we are now able to completely pay for ten soldiers a year to come here."

I'm still in shock staring at the dollar amount in front of me. That's over three months of operating expenses for this place, and we could do so much with that money.

Leaning in, I give Levi a short kiss before standing up.

"I'm going to get going on this budget. With the first of the month just a few days away, we've got to have it nailed down."

"Hey," he grabs my hand to get my attention. "Will you stop by and see me before you leave for the day?"

"Yeah, but it could be very late."

"That's fine. I just want to see you before you go, and I'm generally up pretty late, anyway."

Leaving, I go down to my office and get to work on the budget. Until there's a soft knock on my door, I haven't looked up from my computer. Looking up, I find Lexi standing there.

"It's past dinnertime, and I know you haven't left your office, so I brought you some food." She holds up a plate.

Taking a break from the computer, I roll my shoulders and stretch my neck. Until now, I hadn't realized how little I had actually moved in the past few hours.

"How are you feeling?" I ask Lexi. "I know you're still getting morning sickness, but other than that?"

"Other than that, I'm feeling good. Even though I'm really excited about this party to tell everyone finally, I hate having to keep hiding it. When I had to lie to my parents about being sick and missing dinner last weekend, they wanted to come check on me, but Noah told them it wasn't worth them getting sick over."

"Well, the party is next weekend, so not too much longer. Use me as an excuse if you need to, but text me what your cover story is, and I'll happily back it up."

That earns me a laugh before she turns around to leave, but she pauses.

"Well, don't work too late. I know you've been putting in a lot of hours, but you need sleep, too."

"Isn't that what coffee is for?"

She smiles and shakes her head but heads out, I'm sure to go home to Noah. It's easy to say not to work so late when you have someone to go home to. When you have an empty house like me, it's not always a big draw.

After putting in another few hours of work, I decide to call it a day. Checking the clock, I see it's almost eleven at night, but I want to see if, by some chance, Levi happens to be awake. I grab my stuff, close my office, and make my way upstairs.

Oakside's different at night. It's quiet and calm. There's no one in the lobby, and it's like the entire building is asleep. As I head down the hallway, I can still see a light on in Levi's room. His door is closed, so I knock lightly, hoping that if he has drifted off with the light on that I won't wake him.

"Come in; it's open," he calls from the other side.

Cracking open the door, I slip in, closing it behind me. I find him sitting on the couch in sweatpants and a T-shirt. Ace is lying on the couch as well with his head in Levi's lap, and they are watching TV together.

"I really thought you'd be asleep by now," I say as I join him on the couch. When I rest my head on his shoulder, he wraps his arm around me, and it's like a wall of exhaustion hits me all at once.

"I told you I stay up pretty late. On deployments, I had a lot of night shifts, and my schedule never really flipped around."

He gently rubs my arm, and we sit and watch some comedy sitcom he has on. The next thing I know, he's gently shaking me to wake me up.

"Mandy, sweetheart, you fell asleep while we were watching TV."

Groaning, I rub my eyes and stretch. I guess I was a lot more tired than I realized I was. Then I gather my purse, figuring I better head home.

"Mandy, you're exhausted."

"Yeah, so I better go home and try to get some sleep."

"No, you are in no condition to drive. Stay here with me. Get some sleep, then go home in the morning and get changed and ready for work." He takes my hand like he's going to fight me on not letting me even leave the room.

I have to admit I like the idea of cuddling up next to his strong body. And better yet, I really like the idea of going back to sleep because I am exhausted. Maybe I should talk to Lexi about putting a couch in my office for nights like this.

Though I hesitate a moment because spending the night in relationships is a big deal. Sex is not on the table because I am just plain exhausted, but it is still another step for us.

"I have a pair of sweatpants you can use, and I'll even let you wear one of my T-shirts." Levi tries to sweeten the deal.

"Sold."

Levi maneuvers himself into his wheelchair and then goes to his dresser and hands me some clothes.

"Use the bathroom and get dressed and ready for bed. I'm going to take Ace out to go to the bathroom for the night."

I take my time in the bathroom, enjoying the smell of him on his clothes. Making sure that I look somewhat sexy after a long day of work is not that easy. I use a bit of his toothpaste on my finger to brush my teeth and figure this is about as good as it's going to get.

Folding up my clothes, I step out of the bathroom. I set my clothes with my purse on the coffee table and turn and find him already in bed. Ace is in his doggy bed right next to Levi's side of the bed.

When I slide into bed, Levi pulls me to his side. It doesn't go unnoticed that it's what he refers to as his good leg that's beside me.

"Goodnight, Levi. Thank you for letting me stay tonight," I say around a yawn.

"Like there would be any chance I'd pass up the opportunity to hold you all night long."

I feel so safe in his arms, but in the back of my mind I know that this is just another step down a path that I can't turn back from. Taking the relationship further before I tell Rebecca what's going on, I know that this is going to end badly one way or another.

# Chapter 14

As I wake up, I realize that someone is in bed beside me, but then it all comes rushing back. Mandy stopped in and fell asleep on the couch, too tired to drive home, so she slept here in bed with me.

Opening my eyes. I take a good look at her. She's lying on my chest and curled up to my side. She's still asleep, and her dirty blonde hair is a slight mess, and she looks so peaceful that I don't even want to move and chance waking her up.

Apparently, Ace doesn't like all my focus being on her because he starts pushing my hand with his nose to get my attention. A glance at the clock shows it's probably time for him to go out for his morning bathroom run.

Reluctantly, I slip out from cuddling with Mandy, and thankfully, it doesn't seem to wake her up. Then as quietly as possible, I maneuver myself to my wheelchair and take Ace out to relieve himself. My nighttime nurse is standing in the hallway, and I know they're getting ready to switch shifts. Spotting me, she winks but doesn't say anything. Meaning that she knows Mandy had spent the night.

In the courtyard waiting on Ace to do his business, I think about Mandy and how right it felt to wake up with her in my arms. With all that's going on, I wonder what the chances are I can get her to do it again. Like Ace can tell that my thoughts are not on him, he brings me a stick to throw, and we play fetch for a few minutes, me tossing the stick across the courtyard and him running to get it and bringing it back to me.

After about ten rounds, he brings the stick, drops it in the dirt, and sits by the door leading back inside. Taking my cue, we go in, and just as we are getting into the room, Mandy is sitting up and rubbing her eyes.

"I was hoping to slip back into bed without waking you," I tell her.

She smiles at me shyly before starting to fix her hair. I don't bother to tell her not to worry about it because I love the *just woke up* look on her, but I know that she'll still worry about it, anyway.

We stare at each other for a few moments before she stirs again. Both of us look at the clock and see it just before seven a.m.

"I guess I should get dressed and go home so I can get ready for work and not be late," she says, though there's a reluctance in her voice saying that's not what she wants to do.

"Why don't you wear those clothes home? I like the idea of you wearing me to bed at night." I smirk at her, and it does exactly as I hoped it would. A faint blush appears, coating not just her cheeks, but her neck as well.

But she smiles and nods as she starts to gather her stuff. Then she leans down and gives me a kiss on the cheek.

"Since I didn't go home last night, I won't have anything to make us for lunch. But if you're good with your PT today, I'll go to my favorite deli in town and get us some lunch," she says.

"Only if you let me buy," I say, giving her a stern look, letting her know that I'm not budging on this.

Instead of going to the door and home as I expected, she sits down with an almost defeated look on her face.

"Before I do anything, I have to call Rebecca. I'm going to set up a meeting with her and tell her what's going on because I can't hide this from her anymore."

I move my chair right in front of her, reach over and take both her hands in mine.

"Yes, it's time to tell her, but you telling her doesn't change anything between us. Tell me you know that." While she doesn't say anything, she does nod but is looking down at her hands.

I tilt her head up to look at me before speaking again.

"I need your words. Tell me that you know no matter what happens between you and Rebecca, that it changes nothing between us."

"I know that whatever happens between Rebecca and me it will not change anything between us," she says it, but she doesn't have any heart behind those words.

That's okay, I have plenty of time to show her that I mean it, and maybe that's what she needs, actions over words.

"But what if she wants to see you? We both know that when she finds out you're here injured, she's going to be here faster than lightning."

Though she doesn't say it, I can hear uncertainty and maybe even a bit of irritation in her voice. I think for a moment how I would feel if she was injured and one of her ex-boyfriends rushed to her side, and I had no way of controlling it.

Just the thought of one of her ex-boyfriends at her side strikes up a flash of anger in me. I want to be the one to help her and take care of her. They left her and they don't get that privilege anymore. Is this how she feels about the idea of Rebecca rushing to my side?

Things between Mandy and me are still pretty new, and neither of us has been in a hurry to push things forward or stake a claim on anything. For that reason, I haven't been in a rush to analyze my feelings, but what I feel for her is strong.

"You tell her that I'm not allowing any visitors right now. And as of this morning, that will be true. Then you tell her you will set up a double date with her and her husband and you and me."

When she hesitantly looks at me with hope and her eyes finally lock on mine, the sweet smile which spreads over her face makes my heart leap in my chest. If I wasn't in love with this girl before, that winsome smile has assured me that I am now.

Tugging the back of her neck to me, I pull her in for a kiss because if I don't, the words I don't want to say right now might slip from my mouth. I know that I'll scare her and send her running. Before we take that step, I know she needs time and has to work things out with Rebecca. But hell, I'm ready.

When the kiss is over, she stands, gathers her things, and at the doorway, she looks at me with another smile.

"After your PT appointment, I'll stop by and see how it went and we'll decide on lunch. Before then, I'll call Rebecca, so I'll be able to let you know how it goes."

Then she's gone, and the room seems to lose its shine and it is too empty without her. Ace seems to sense my thoughts because he rests his head on my lap. To comfort both of us, I reach down and pet him. A moment later, Kaitlyn walks in with a big smile on her face.

She goes through her morning routine of checking my vitals, asking if I'm in any pain, and how I'm doing. Then she reminds me of my schedule for the day, my appointments, and anything else I need to know.

"Could you have Noah stop by and see me when he gets in? I need to talk to him about something that's important?" I ask as she gets ready to leave.

"He just got here. I'll send him right in."

Then I go into the bathroom and get ready for the day. When I come out, Noah is sitting on the couch waiting for me.

"Everything okay? I was told you needed to talk to me, and it was important."

"Yeah, is it possible to put no visitors down for me other than Mandy, Kade, and the people here?"

My request makes Noah sit up straight and look at me.

"Of course. Is everything okay?"

"I don't know how much Mandy has told you or even Lexi, and I don't want her to be mad at me for this, but Mandy's best friend is my ex-girlfriend." Noah's eyes go wide, so I know he's understanding what I'm saying.

"Mandy's had trouble telling her about us, but she's resolved to call her and set up a meeting or I don't know, tell her over the phone possibly. But my ex is the type of girl that when she hears I'm hurt, she'll attempt to see me and she can be overbearing. All of this worries Mandy and I think it would just be better all the way around that she's not able to visit. Plus, I really don't want to see my family either if they happen to find out I'm here and try to show up."

"Consider it done. As soon as I go back to my desk, I'll put it in the system. Now the rumor is that you had a visitor last night," he smirks at me. News travels fast here, and it's almost worse than small-town gossip.

"Yeah, Mandy stopped by to see me before she left last night. It was late and when she sat down, less than a minute later, she was asleep on my shoulder. I didn't feel comfortable with her driving like that, so I suggested that she stay here. Is that all right?"

I'm not sure what the rules are, but I would assume with Mandy being friends with his wife that he would have her best interests at heart as well.

"It's more than okay. Of course, we don't want her driving if she's too tired. For a while, I'd been debating about adding a set of bunk beds into the staff room. We've had a couple of nurses pull a double shift and I thought maybe if they were able to get a nap before heading home, I'd feel more comfortable."

"Honestly, it couldn't hurt or even a couch for someone to crash on if they need to."

Noah nods and then with a few short goodbyes he heads out, I'm sure to update my request in the system. With about thirty minutes before my PT appointment, I grab Ace's favorite ball and take him with me out to the front porch to throw it around and let him run off some of his energy.

Once Ace realizes that we are going outside, it's like a switch goes off and he starts jumping and dancing around like we can't get there fast enough. The only time we come out to the front porch is for him to run and catch the ball, and it's something that we both love.

I park my chair at the edge of the porch and lock the wheels. Ace sits in the grass in front of me and watches my every move. When I look at him, he stands on all fours and I show him the ball. Then I throw it and he watches it at an odd angle to make sure his eye is able to watch the ball before he takes off running and catches it in midair.

"All right, buddy, that one wasn't an easy one," I say, petting his head as he brings me the ball. Running out in front of me, he once again keeps his eye on the ball. This time I throw it much further and he chases after it. The front lawn is at a bit of a downward slope, so once the ball hits the ground, it rolls for a good bit. He has a blast, this being one of his favorite things to do.

As he's bringing the ball back, a car pulls up the driveway. I'm sure it's some staff getting ready for the day. Then I throw the ball again and as Ace is bringing it to me, Mandy steps onto the porch on the far side over by where the staff park.

She looks hot as hell in jeans, a light pink silk top, and boots that come up to her ankle and have a little heel. I can't take my eyes off of her, even with Ace returning and laying the ball in my lap.

"Hot date?" I joke with her, but she smiles and shakes her head.

"I figured if I had to call Rebecca that dressing up would give me some extra confidence."

"You haven't talked to her yet? When I told Noah, he had my visitor restrictions put in place and is now active."

"No, my plan is to go do it now from my office because Lexi can be my person to interrupt me if I have to end the call quickly. She's already there and has agreed to be my SOS."

Ace starts to get impatient about me throwing the ball again, so she leans down and pets him, and then squeezes my shoulder.

"Have a good appointment, and I'll see you soon." Then she kisses my cheek before going inside.

After tossing the ball a few more times, it's time to head in for my appointment. Our activity seems to have tired Ace out because once we're in the PT room, he curls up in his favorite spot by the waiting room chairs and passes out.

"What did you do to that poor dog? He couldn't be more tired," Vince laughs.

"We were just out on the front porch, and I was throwing a ball around for him, trying to kill a little bit of his energy."

Then, just like that, we launch into working with my prosthetic. He has me up and walking with the bars to steady myself and by the end, I'm even able to take a few laps with a walker. My leg is sore but a good kind of sore.

"You should start wearing the prosthetic a little more each day as you get used to it. Use the walker around your room, but only under supervision, at least for the next week or until you're more stable."

I'm nodding along because while I hear everything he says, my mind is already whirling with the thought of how much more freedom I'll have.

Even if it means pushing the boundaries just a little bit, I'm determined to get used to this prosthetic sooner rather than later.

# Chapter 15

## Mandy

Sitting down at my desk, I stare at my phone like it's a snake that's going to bite me. It's funny how I think I can't live without my phone until I have to make a phone call that I really don't want to make.

After taking a few more deep breaths, I pick up the phone and dial Rebecca's number. It rings a few times before she picks up.

"Hey Mandy, everything okay? It's kind of early."

"Yeah, do you have a minute to chat?"

"For you always. I was up early and made Dale some breakfast before he went to work. Now, I'm just being lazy on the couch, so I have all the time that you need."

"Well, I just got into work, so I only have a few minutes," I say, setting the stage for being interrupted if needed. Of course, that's when Lexi peeks her head in and nods, and stands there, ready to be my rescuer if needed. God, I love that girl.

Taking another deep breath, I decide that if I'm going to do this, I should at least do this in person. Rebecca deserves that.

"So, I have something kind of important that I really need to talk to you about. And I was hoping that maybe I could come up and you and I could have lunch this weekend. I'm off Sunday."

Rebecca hesitates for only a moment before answering, "Girl, you are welcome up here anytime and you don't need an excuse to come have lunch with me. Dale will be working and there is this amazing Italian place that just opened up a couple of blocks from the house. How about I order takeout and we can eat here at the house?"

"That sounds perfect. If I leave here by nine, I'll be up there no later than noon."

"All right, I'll see you then. Go get to work, so you don't get in trouble, or they make you work this weekend to make up for it," she laughs.

We say our goodbyes, and I hang up, and Lexi just looks at me.

"Rebecca and I have been friends for almost ten years. No matter the outcome, I really think she deserves to be told this face to face. But she is pregnant, so if I come in with a black eye, you'll know why." I try to make a joke of it, but Lexi isn't smiling.

"It's just you are putting it off for another day and you can't keep doing that. But let's push it out of our heads because Friday is the surprise party to tell everyone. Noah's family gets in on Thursday, and they are telling Noah that it's just an excuse to have his sister see the Savannah college and for them to be there for his birthday."

"What a double life you lead," and we both erupt into giggles. This whole surprise party could go wrong or it could go right, but so far Lexi has been able to hide their secret and now they only have a couple more days to do so.

Lexi is right though. Focusing on the party is the best way to not think too hard about my visit with Rebecca. Once I'm alone again in the office, I get to work trying to kill time during Levi's PT appointment. Even though I want to be up in his room waiting to hear about the appointment from the moment he gets there, I don't want to come off as the clingy girl either.

Though I have work to do, I try to concentrate on it, but the time seems to drag on. When it's finally lunchtime, I close everything down, grab my purse, and go to Levi's room. He should have been out of his PT appointment for at least an hour, so it's the perfect time for me to go grab lunch and spend a little time with him before getting back to work.

I find him in his room sitting on the couch, and the new addition to his room is the walker on the other side of his wheelchair.

"Did Vince give you homework?" I ask in a way of asking how his appointment was.

"Yeah, we're working on me practicing walking around a bit."

"Well, let me go grab our lunch, and then you can tell me all about it."

Levi hands me some money for lunch and even though it makes me a little uncomfortable, I let him do it. We don't get to date like a normal couple, so things have to be done a little differently for us. And I'm fine with that.

With Oakside being in the small town of Clark Springs, Georgia, it doesn't take long to get into town and to the deli, which is only one of about three places to eat in town. Even though it's lunchtime and what would be considered the lunch rush anywhere else, there's only one other person in line ahead of me.

In less than twenty minutes I'm back in Levi's room, spreading out our lunch on the coffee table.

"So, I called Rebecca," I say, deciding that I want to get this out there first so that we can enjoy the rest of our lunch.

Levi studies my face for a moment and then reaches over and takes my hand.

"How did it go?"

"Since Rebecca and I have known each other so long, I decided that at the very least I should tell her this face to face. Then if she wants to, it would give her the chance to punch me in the face. So, we are having lunch together on Sunday."

"That's fair. But I will warn you if you chicken out this time, I'll call her and tell her myself."

I start to smile and then freeze. Levi has her number. Have they been talking? Have they still been in contact since he went away to boot camp?

"Stop whatever is racing around in your mind. I have not had contact with Rebecca since we broke up. But I do have an old social media profile, and she was one of the few people that sent me a friend request before I abandoned it a few years ago. It wouldn't be hard to get online and send her a message to get her phone number."

The thought of Rebecca and Levi talking again makes me very uneasy. They have so much more history together and even though Rebecca is married, I shouldn't be worried. Yet I still am.

We finish our lunch, staying on much safer topics like how his PT appointment went and his plans to go out to the back porch and let Ace run around and get some fresh air.

Then I tell him more about Noah's party coming up. When I ask him to join me, he agrees. Even though they do want to still keep it a small intimate event, I guess the more people that we can get there who are friends, the more it won't look like they have something else planned.

After lunch, I go back to my office and get some more work done. The whole time I keep getting distracted with thoughts of Levi and Rebecca talking. They never really wanted to break up but felt like they didn't have any other choice with her going off to college, and him going off to boot camp.

When they couldn't promise they would see each other regularly, and they didn't want to do the whole long-distance thing, it was the end. His time off was when she was in school, and her time was off was when he would be in boot camp.

Eventually, they both moved on, and Rebecca dated quite a few guys before she met Dale her senior year at her internship. The moment her internship ended, Dale asked her out, and they were engaged a year later. Married a year after that and now that they've been married a year and they're expecting their first little one. I don't think I've ever seen her happier.

So why is the thought of her talking to Levi bothering me so much?

By dinnertime, I give up the fight of trying to work and decide to go see how Levi's doing. After that, I'm going over to Noah and Lexi's to finish up any last-minute plans before his family gets into town.

When I get up to Levi's room instead of finding him on the couch watching TV, he's lying in bed with the TV going, but he's not really watching it.

I walk over to the bed and kneel down so that we are face to face.

"What's wrong?"

He groans, "Just in a lot of pain. I guess I overdid it at PT."

His dark brown hair has gotten longer, and I brush it off his forehead.

If it was from PT, wouldn't he have been sore at lunch? "What did you do after I left?"

"I did the exercises that Vince told me to do."

Staring at him, I feel like there's something he's not telling me, and I'm about to let it go when he cries out again.

"I may have pushed myself too hard and done too many of the exercises."

"Oh, Levi, why would you do that? You probably set yourself back instead of helping yourself."

"You should go. I'm just going to go to sleep early. Hopefully, I'll feel better in the morning."

"Hey, don't push me away." He's not even looking at me right now, and I don't like it.

"You're not going to like my reasoning for doing it, so it's not even worth bringing up," he says and finally opens his eyes enough to look into mine.

In his eyes, I see a lot of pain, and I can't even imagine what he's going through.

"You can tell me anything; you know that, right?"

"I did this for you."

Feeling like I've just been slapped, I jerk backward. "How is this for me? I don't like seeing you in pain."

"You deserve a man that can take you out on a date, that can hold your hand, and go for a walk. I did this so that I could get used to my prosthetic faster and be a real man for you."

"What have I done to make you feel like I need any of that?"

My brain starts tracking back over the last few days. What could I have possibly done to make him feel that way?

"Nothing, but you're going to feel that way eventually. No woman is going to want a cripple for a boyfriend or much less anything else in her life for a very long."

"Damn it, Levi, if you weren't in bed already in pain, I'd slap you across your damn face! How dare you? Do you really think that little of me? I don't care if you're in a wheelchair or running marathons. All I see is a man who makes me laugh, listens when I need to talk, and who gives me butterflies when he gives me that sexy look from across the room."

Before I say something that I'm going to regret, I stand and go to the door.

"Mandy..." he says, calling after me.

"No, I'm going to go. For the record, you didn't need two legs to do all those things, and it didn't take two legs to get me to start falling for you either."

I turn, walking out, I give his nurse a heads up on his pain and then don't stop until I'm over at Lexi and Noah's, or rather I collapse on the bench on the front porch where they're both sitting waiting on me.

"Oh, what happened?" Lexi asks.

I take a minute and then tell her about my conversation with Levi. Noah wastes no time and gets his nurse on the phone, along with his doctor, to check on him.

"Relationships aren't easy," Lexi says. "But relationships with guys here at Oakside are even harder. On their bad days, they want to push everyone away and they will. But when they start to feel better, they'll start to regret it. Just go easy on him, because until he starts to make peace with himself, he's not going to understand how anyone else can be at peace with him."

Easier said than done.

# Chapter 16

## Noah

Today is the day of the big surprise party. I may be at Oakside to work, but work is the last thing on my mind. My parents just got in last night with my sisters, and they're here helping Lexi decorate for the party.

This morning, Mom kicked me out of the house with the story of wanting some girl time which apparently included my father. Mandy and Paisley went over to help with decorations as well, and things are going good from the texts that I have gotten.

When they're done decorating, my parents and my sisters are going to come here, and we are going to have lunch. They think their job is to keep me occupied while everybody arrives at the house. That's partly true, but this is also when Lexi, Mandy, and Paisley will decorate the sunroom with the details for the surprise announcement that we're pregnant.

Then we'll keep that room hidden until after they think they've surprised me with my birthday party. I've been going over the details in my head, wanting to make sure that we get it just right because this is probably the biggest surprise that I'll ever be able to give my parents.

For Lexi as well, I also know that this is a big thing. For a while, she didn't think that kids were in her future. Then she met me, and everything changed, so I want to make sure that this goes off without a hitch for her.

Knowing that Levi overdid it the other day, I head down to his room to peek my head in wanting to make sure that he's doing better. When I get to his room, he's on the couch watching TV. I lightly knock on his door, and he nods when he sees it's me.

He guesses the reason that I'm there right away and makes no effort to hide the fact that he's beyond irritated right now.

"See, I'm sitting here on the couch like a good boy doing what I'm told, taking it easy. I'm bored out of my mind and feel like I could be moving forward, but here I am stuck on the couch."

"I know it doesn't feel like it, but you're resting and letting your leg heal which is moving forward. You aren't the first guy to finally find his motivation to push himself and get out of here. Also, you aren't the first one to be motivated and push too hard, and you won't be the last."

"It just sucks. I'm ready to be out of here and to move forward with my life."

"While I completely understand, you may not see it, but I can tell you that you are doing so much better than when you first got here. When we brought you in, you wanted nothing to do with your prosthetic. But you're learning to walk on it, and what's more, you want to walk on it. You've learned to maneuver yourself in and out of bed or go pretty much anywhere, but you haven't let the fact that you've lost your leg stop you."

"But?"

"But you need to start talking to your therapist. Before you're discharged, he has to sign off. Doesn't matter if you master walking around with your prosthetic. If your therapist doesn't sign off on you leaving, then you don't go. Just because you're excelling at one part of your treatment, don't ignore this one."

Even though he looks away from me and starts watching TV again, I know this is all stuff that he's been told but eventually will sink in. I decide it's best to let him be and walk to the lobby. As I stand in the doorway, I just take in everything that Lexi and I have built.

I didn't live here very long before this place was turned into Oakside as we know it now, but it's such a vast difference. When Lexi started talking about her vision, I could see it right along with her. It was so infectious, and she made it come true.

I know better than any of these guys what a dramatic turn your life can take. I had planned to retire from the military, marry Whitney, and have a family with her, but after the explosion, everything went up in smoke, literally. Whitney dumped me, and with all the scarring, I thought my life was basically over.

That's the moment Lexi walked in, and I don't even like to think about what my life would be like if she hadn't. Every morning, I still wake up shocked that this is my life and grateful that it is.

"I thought I was the one with the reputation of staring off into space," Easton says, coming to lean on the wall beside me.

"My parents are here spending time with Lexi, and I've been banished here to get some work done. But to say that my mind just isn't here would be an understatement." I'm trying to stick as close to the truth as possible because I don't like the idea of lying to Easton.

We'll be surprising him at the party as well, assuming Paisley hasn't already spilled the beans. But if she has, he will at least act surprised.

"It's always dangerous when the in-laws get together with the spouse. Not that I have anything to compare it to, but I do tend to get into trouble with my father-in-law mighty often," he chuckles.

Silently, we both stare into space for a few minutes before he pushes himself up off the wall.

"Well," Easton says, "Why don't you go make your rounds in the dining room and say hi to everyone? I'm sure there's someone there that will have a story to tell you to keep you occupied."

He's right, of course. The next hour and a half fly by, and the next thing I know my family is standing in the dining room doorway ready to have lunch with me. Saying my goodbyes to the man that I'm talking to, I go and join them.

"So today we are having an Italian-themed lunch. There are different kinds of pasta to choose from and everyone's favorite lasagna too. Also, there's some garlic bread and even some tiramisu for dessert," I say, greeting them all with a hug.

Both of my sisters' eyes light up at the mention of dessert, which is exactly why I asked the chef to include it. As we're getting our food, I decide with it being such a nice day that we should eat out on the back porch.

"How do you guys feel about eating outside?"

They all agree, so I lead them out to the back porch, and we take a table off to the side so that we won't be disturbed.

During lunch, I talk to my sister, Lucy, about her photography, and if she's excited about the possibility of going to school here. My sister, Grace, who loves to cook and bake, tells me about the most recent recipes that she's tried out.

My dad tells me about his new job, and my mom relates all the gossip and info about everybody at home. We've long since finished our lunches and are just sitting there visiting when my phone rings. It's Lexi and I know that this is our signal that everything is in place.

"Hello?" I answer the phone.

Like Lexi said she would, she delivers her excuse in case anyone could hear her.

"Hey baby, there's something here that I need your help with. I thought that your parents and your sisters would like to maybe watch a movie with me. Do you guys want to come back here?"

"Hang on, let me ask them."

Since I already know that they're aware of why Lexi is calling, but they don't think that I am, so I follow my lines.

"Lexi suggested that we go back over there. She'd like to watch a movie with you all. How does that sound?"

Smiling, they nod and agree.

"That sounds good. We're just finishing up lunch, so we'll be over there in about fifteen minutes."

To get the timing right, I know Lexi will be stalking my location on her phone, so I don't make her wait. After I get everything cleaned up, we walk down the path between Oakside and our house.

Once there, we step onto the front porch, but everyone stands back in order to make sure I'm the first one in the door. I know as soon as I go through this door, everyone is going to yell surprise. But I've been working on my surprised face even though Lexi says that it leaves something to be desired.

Just like planned, I opened the door, and everyone yells, and the lights in the house flip on. I jump back acting surprised, and then start laughing, and everybody comes up to hug me.

Lexi's parents are here, along with her brother, sister-in-law, and their son. Also, I see Easton and Paisley, along with Mandy and Levi. Even our nurses, who have turned into friends, Kaitlyn and Brooke, are both here.

After saying hello to everyone my eyes find Lexi's and she nods.

"So," Lexi starts, "since this is the first time that we've had both Noah's parents and my parents in the same place at the same time, we wanted to do something a little special for you. Will you join me in the sunroom?"

Both sets of parents look at the other to see if anyone had any idea what was going on. But since they don't, they follow Lexi. Then I turned to the rest of our guests. "There's a little surprise for you guys as well." I go behind the parents and everyone follows behind me.

Lexi waits until I am within eyesight before she opens the door to the sunroom, and both sets of parents step in with Johnny and Becky not far behind them. The moment they see what we've arranged, there are all sorts of happy screams and excitement. Then they turn back and look at us.

What they see are baby shower decorations everywhere with a banner that says, 'you are going to be grandparents.'

"You're pregnant?" my mom asks, and when Lexi nods, both mothers wrapped her in a hug.

Then both of our dads shake my hand before mine reaches over and each hug Lexi as well. By this time, the rest of our guests start to see everything, and everyone gets really excited about the news.

It's a good twenty minutes before everybody settles down, and everyone filters back into the kitchen. Finally, I am able to make my way over to my wife, wrapping my arms around her and pulling her in close for just a minute.

"How are you feeling? All this decorating and planning today didn't take too much out of you, did it?"

"Actually, it was lots of fun, and I've been looking forward to it. I think we really surprised them and that's the best part."

"No. The best part is this amazing gift that you're giving me. Growing our child and everything that you're going through is the best present. I'm in awe of you every day, my Angel."

I tip her head up and kiss her, showing exactly how I feel. Every single day, I want to make sure she knows how much she and this child mean to me, and I will do whatever I have to for them.

"Now that the cat is out of the bag, I want you to take it easier at work. I put a couch in our office and another one in the staff room, so if you get tired, I want you to lie down. Whenever you can, I want you to put your feet up." I tell her.

"That sounds amazing. But you do know I plan on working as long as I possibly can. Right?"

"I know, but if I had it my way, you would lie in bed and do nothing but binge Hallmark movies all day and be pampered endlessly."

"Well, I reserve the right to take you up on that towards the end of my pregnancy when I'm starting to feel miserable."

It's an open invitation, and she knows that. Hell, I'd be happy to pamper her even if she wasn't pregnant. All she'd have to do is let me.

Neither of us knows what the future holds, but I do know that Lexi is *my* miracle and this little one will be *our* miracle.

Changes are coming to Oakside, not just because Lexi is pregnant, but we have a lot going on. I just hope all the change is the good kind.

# Chapter 17

## Levi

I'm still reeling from my fight with Mandy. She had invited me to Noah's party, and I went, but the entire time she found plenty of ways to avoid me. There was always someone else to talk to or something she promised Lexi she would do. I could tell she was still upset, and I didn't blame her.

All I can think about before going to bed is that fight and how it was my own insecurities that got the better of me.

"Do you have a minute? There's something I'd like to talk to you about," Noah says, and when I nod, he closes the door behind him.

I hadn't even realized he was standing there until he spoke. I guess this thing with Mandy is on my mind more than I realized. Noah sits down in the chair next to me, and I turn the TV off, waiting for him to speak.

"So, the girls don't even know that I'm here. Don't get mad at them, but I heard Mandy and Lexi talking, and I'm going to stick my nose in where it probably doesn't belong. But I wanted a chance to talk to you," he says, giving me a sheepish smile.

"I guess it's not the best-kept secret that Mandy and I are fighting, huh?"

"I think it was only obvious to those of us that know you. But I think every person that passes through this place has the same fears and the same thoughts that you do, even if we never really speak to them out loud. Some of us don't even admit them to ourselves."

He pulls out his phone and starts flipping through it before handing it to me. The photo on the screen shocks me. It's Noah, but not as he looks now. There are so many more scars on his face, and he's lying in a hospital bed. The one side of his face is covered in scars, ugly, nasty ones raising the skin. Some are pink and white, and part of his ear is missing.

"That was me before I had the plastic surgeries. I had just gotten the bandages off, and I didn't ever want to look at myself in the mirror. But every day, Lexi looked at me, tracing over my scars, memorizing them."

He lifts up the side of his shirt, showing me his stomach. Those same scars travel down all one side of him. Now I get why he's always pretty covered even on the hottest days.

"I was burned down the entire side of my body. Those scars go from my face to my foot. When I met Lexi, I was all bandaged up and had no idea how bad it really was. Having her around was more of a distraction from the pain, at least in the little time that I was conscious between doses of the pain medication."

Then he shows me another picture of him and Lexi sitting on a couch that you can tell is taken in the hospital. He still has all the scars and while he's not smiling, Lexi is, but there's a hint of sadness around her eyes.

"That was right before I went in for the first of what was many surgeries. At that moment, I also knew Lexi was so much more than just a distraction, even if I thought she would never feel the same way about me. Here's something else that many people don't know, I was told by the doctor that due to the burns there was a chance I may never have kids. Actually, they weren't even sure if I'd even be able to get hard again, and were convinced that some of the nerves down there had been affected."

I can't even imagine having that kind of stress on top of everything else. While I know from first-hand experience that sex is the last thing on your mind when you're going through everything, and you're trying to heal. But I've always known in the back of my head that it would be a part of my life again, in one form or another. Having to come to terms with it never being part of your life again on top of everything else that you're dealing with, well, I couldn't even imagine.

"Lexi never gave up on me though, and we had fun experimenting. Over time it did happen, almost like a muscle which needed to strengthen. One way or another, I was too scared to know, and I used it as a way to push Lexi away, though she didn't let me."

And now, after all that he'd dealt with, he's going to be a dad with the girl that was there for him through it all.

"How did you push past the thought of not being the man that she needs? There was always that possibility you wouldn't be able to take care of her like she wanted or in the way that you wanted to be able to." I ask.

"Actually, I suggested an open relationship, so that she would get her needs met elsewhere. But for her, that was a deal-breaker."

He chuckles, almost lost in his memories before continuing, "She actually told me that my hands worked just fine."

"Yeah, she sounds a lot like Mandy," I say without even really thinking.

"It takes a strong woman to be by a man at his lowest point. And I think at some time in our relationship, we all try to push them away. I did it with Lexi, Easton did it with Paisley, and I've seen countless other couples go through the same thing no matter how long they've been together. It's one of the ultimate tests on a relationship."

"So, this is just the long, drawn out way of you telling me that I was an idiot and I need to suck it up and apologize to Mandy?"

Without saying the words, Noah stares at me for a moment. I guess he's telling me that I know exactly what he meant.

"Mandy will not be in tomorrow and she went home early today. She's heading to her friend Rebecca's house tomorrow for lunch. Apparently, they have something to talk about."

Oh yeah, they have something to talk about all right.

*Me*.

# Chapter 18

## Mandy

Normally, I like to enjoy the ride to Rebecca's house. Cranking up the music, I sing along and let the drive calm me. Today relaxing seems to be the last thing I'm able to do. The closer I get, the more butterflies seem to multiply in my stomach.

I have a million different excuses on why I shouldn't tell her. Ranging from she's happily married, so it shouldn't matter, to she's pregnant and I don't want to stress her out, and finally, it's just not the right time.

But when I think about any of the excuses, then I think about telling Levi that's the reason that I didn't tell her, and it just doesn't sit well with me. Part of me needs to know if this is going to be an issue and another part of me needs to get it taken care of so we can move on.

As I turn into her neighborhood of fancy houses with perfectly manicured lawns, I start taking a few deep breaths. When I pull into her driveway, I don't even get the car in park before the front door opens, which makes me think that she was waiting by the front window for me. Does she know something's wrong?

"Mandy!" she squeals as she comes and gives me a hug.

It hasn't been that long since I've seen her, but her belly has already grown noticeably bigger. But I know better than to say that to a pregnant woman, so I just hug her back.

"It's such a nice day that I thought we would eat out on the back porch. It's screened in, so we don't have to worry about bugs. Dale's mom gave me her fried chicken recipe and for whatever reason, I have been craving nothing but fried chicken this entire pregnancy. I've been eating every brand I can, but I keep coming back to his mom's and he finally got the recipe from her," she rambles on as we go inside.

"Rebecca, stop and take a deep breath. Eating outside is fine and whatever you have to cook, even if it's just sandwiches, is great. I'm just here to spend some time with you."

"Yes, but I know you have something to talk to me about, and not knowing what it is makes me nervous."

It's hard to forget how well we know each other. We never really kept secrets growing up because the other one always knew when there was a secret, so it didn't stay that way long. On the drive here, I reasoned that I would have to tell her because she'd dig it out of me. Besides, I don't think she will let me out of here without telling her what's going on.

She goes to the kitchen and starts pulling food from the warmer.

"Here, give that to me and let me take it out to the table," I say as she hands me the food. Then she turns to get us some drinks from the refrigerator.

Heading out to the back porch, I find the table set with some brightly colored dishes and napkins. I can't help but smile because it just screams Rebecca. My smile widens even more when I notice that the plates and the napkins match the chairs and furniture that are out on the back porch.

Rebecca has always been one of those people that love to decorate and match things. If I know her like I think I do, I'm pretty sure that these plates are specifically her back porch plates, and not the same ones that she would use at the dining room table inside the house.

I laugh to myself as I take a seat, and she steps out onto the back porch with a tray of sweet tea.

"Sit down and eat. Tell me what's going on since I saw you in Savannah," I say to her, figuring that I should at least get some food into her before I drop the bomb.

"Well, those meetings in Savannah led to Dale getting a raise and a promotion. The promotion will allow him to work at the main office here. Plus the company is even going to give him three weeks of paternity leave once the baby is born and then he'll be able to use his two weeks' vacation pay to extend on to that time. So he will be home with me for quite a bit which I'm really looking forward to."

As a soon-to-be parent, I can only imagine how stressed she is. It's a whole new world having to raise another human being, but knowing that Dale will be here for her has to be a relief.

"What about you? What's going on at Oakside?"

"Well, Lexi is pregnant, and she just told everybody. It was kind of ingenious the way she did it. She threw what everyone thought was a surprise party for her husband where they turned around and told everyone that they were expecting. So, the energy around Oakside is really high."

"Oh, wouldn't it be great if we both had little girls? I could pass on my clothes to her, and then I wouldn't feel so bad about spending so much money on dresses. Have you seen the price of a dress for a little girl who might wear it for maybe three months? I fell in love with one until I saw it was almost forty dollars. Since she'll only wear it for a short time, which means I might put it on her two or three times. It's crazy."

Even though Dale makes good money, Rebecca grew up on a budget, so she still isn't used to spending money. I think she will make sure that everything matches like out on this porch. I'm willing to bet that everything on the porch she got on sale or on clearance.

"Oh, I'm sure she would appreciate it. Though I don't think they have even started thinking that far ahead. They're very hands-on with Oakside, so I know they're going to have to start planning for when their little one comes, and they can't be there as much as they are now. But if I know Lexi, she'll probably just strap the baby in a baby carrier on her chest and continue going.

Rebecca laughs at that, and for a moment I want to keep that happy smile there. But Rebecca has eaten about half of her lunch, and I know that I can't keep putting it off, so I take a deep breath and set my fork down. Sensing that something is coming, Rebecca sets her fork down as well and wipes her hands on her napkin.

"I have to tell you something, but I need you to remember that I was not allowed to tell you because even though the men and women at Oakside are not my patients, they still fall under patient confidentiality."

This was something Lexi had told me to say in the event that this backfires on me.

"Okay?" she looks confused, and I'm not surprised.

"Now don't get all worked up and don't jump to conclusions because there's a lot I need to tell you, but Levi is a patient at Oakside." I pause and let it sink in what that means, and it only takes a moment before her eyes go wide and she opens her mouth like she's going to speak again.

"Wait, let me finish. He's been there a little while and hasn't wanted anyone to know where he was. I do have his permission to tell you now, but there is something else that you need to know."

"Is he all right? I should probably go back with you. Can I visit with him? He shouldn't be there alone, and I know his family didn't even want him to join the military, so they're not there for him, are they? Oh, he shouldn't be there by himself. I'm sure Dale will understand."

For just a minute, I squeeze my eyes shut because I knew this would be her reaction.

"He does not want you to come back with me, and he has not been alone. You're right, his family hasn't been there, but I've been there. And that's what I need to talk to you about."

That seems to stop her train of thought as she looks at me. Rebecca is crazy smart. I'm sure the pieces are starting to click together between the guilt that I'm sure is all over my face and the conversation we had in Savannah.

"Levi had been at Oakside for a couple of weeks before I realized that he was there. I had been working late with some budgets and I caught him trying to sneak downstairs for a snack. Once I realized who it was, I began spending time with him each day so he wouldn't be alone. Usually, I'd bring him lunch that wasn't the healthy stuff that Oakside serves."

When her face goes to stone and loses all emotion, I almost stop and start begging for her forgiveness right there. But I know that I need to get the whole story out or I may never get another chance to.

"When I first started hanging out with him, he wasn't thrilled, but he needed someone to help push him to go to his appointments and all. Then we started spending more time together. We didn't plan anything but it kind of happened and we kissed... now he wants to take me out on a date... "

Stunned, she sits there for just a minute and doesn't say anything. Then stands and walks outside on the porch to her backyard to the far side of the yard where she has a small little flower garden. With her back to me, she just stands staring at the flowers.

I have no idea what to do. Should I follow her? Do I give her space? Do I leave?

I pull up my phone and send Lexi a quick text.

**Me**: So, I told her, and she got up and walked outside without saying a word. Do I go after her or what do I do?

**Lexi**: It's hard to say, but I would give her a few minutes and then go see if she wants to talk. Make sure you apologize.

Then I put my phone away as I figure it wouldn't be good for Rebecca to turn and see me on it. Making sure the phone is on silent, I turn and watch Rebecca. She hasn't really moved. She's still standing in the same spot, staring at the same flowers.

Giving her a few more minutes, before I go out to the yard and slowly walk up beside her, making her aware that I'm here without really seeing anything. She turns her head slightly acknowledging that I'm there and that's when I decide to start talking again.

"I'm so sorry. While I didn't mean for any of this to happen, I had to respect his wishes of not telling anyone that he was there."

"I understand, and I'm not upset at you for not telling me that he's there. Though I honestly don't know how I feel. These pregnancy hormones have my emotions all over the place. I want to laugh and cry. I want both of you to be happy, and I'm thankful that you've been there, and he hasn't been alone.

But it's still weird thinking of my best friend dating my ex."

"I know. Had we happened to run into each other, and he asked me out of the blue, my answer would have been no right off the bat because he had dated you. But this kind of snuck up on both of us, which makes it ten times harder for me and probably for you."

When she finally turns back to look at me, her face is soft, and there's a little smile peeking out.

"Levi is a good man. We were just at different points in our life. So, if it happens to work out for you two, I would be thrilled for both of you. But there are certain details you're going to have to keep to a minimum because it is still a little weird."

Giving a small laugh in relief, I'm happy when she wraps her arm around my waist. Then we head back up to the table to finish our lunch. When we sit down again, I have one more detail to bring up before I change the subject.

"There's just one more thing. He knew that you would probably want to visit, and he thought that maybe we could do kind of a double-date lunch. Could you and Dale come down and have lunch with us? He can't leave the facility just yet, so it would have to be at Oakside."

"I'd like that. It'll give me a chance to see where you work, too, so it's a win-win." Then she pauses for a minute before she looks at me with sadness in her eyes. "If he's there, that means he was injured. What happened?"

"I can't tell you much. Mostly because he hasn't told me. He was in an explosion and lost part of his leg from below the knee."

She bows her head over her food for a moment, lost in thought.

"All right then, let's do a double date," she says, and offers me a forced smile.

# Chapter 19

## Mandy

Things with Levi have been tense since our fight two weeks ago. We haven't really talked other than me telling him that Rebecca wanted to set lunch for next week. Before the baby was born, Dale had another trip on the books, and they decided to come for lunch when they were in Savannah.

Though I've been still taking him lunch and cookies every day, I don't really sit and talk with him anymore. It just feels like he doesn't want me in his space. Yet every day that I'm working, I still have this urge to check up on him and make sure he's okay.

Right now, I'm sitting in my office fighting off a headache because I keep stressing about this lunch with Rebecca coming up. Since things with Levi and I are still tense, to say that Rebecca will pick it to death is an understatement.

But it's hard to focus much today, and I'm considering asking Lexi if I can go home early. Maybe I can try to sleep this headache off. When there is a knock on my office door, I look to find Levi standing there.

Yes, standing. He's no longer in his wheelchair, and I have to do a double-take because I wasn't expecting it. Giving me one of his shy smiles, he doesn't say anything, letting me take him in. Of course, Ace is right by his side.

"I was going to take Ace for a walk in the garden and was hoping that maybe you would join us."

Yes, maybe some fresh air will do me good and allow me to focus again on work. So, I nod and open my desk drawer, and take out a few aspirins before joining them. Even though Levi watches me, he doesn't ask any questions.

"I just have a slight headache. Probably from staring at the computer for so long the last few days." I offer so that he won't push the subject.

In silence, we walk with Ace weaving circles around us as we hit the lobby. Once outside, Levi takes a tennis ball from his pocket and throws it across the front lawn. Ace takes off after it. We step off the front porch and start walking towards the garden when he starts to speak.

"I'm really sorry, and I hate how things have been between us. All this is something I still have to come to terms with and it's not easy, but I'm trying." He turns and locks eyes with me. "I'm trying for you."

I'm not really angry at him anymore and haven't been really ever since I got back from Rebecca's house. But I didn't know how he felt, so I just let it be. Not having the words to say what I want to say, I decide instead to reach out for his hand and take it in mine.

Our fingers intertwine and it just feels right. When Ace comes back with the ball, Levi uses his other hand to take the ball and throw it again, closer to the garden this time all without dropping my hand.

"I don't want to push you away, but at the same time, I feel like I should. I'm still trying to comprehend all this, and it's hard to think that you would want to be around me."

Squeezing his hand, I say, "I've been around the men and women here for a while, and I think maybe it's easier for me to accept and deal with because of it. Not only does it take time, but your whole life changed in an instant. It's not just working through learning to walk again; it's coming to terms with what happened. Making an entirely new life plan because the military isn't an option anymore isn't easy. But I wouldn't be here if I didn't want to be."

"I know, and it took me a little while to realize that. I hate how things have been the past couple of weeks with us. But I was hoping maybe you would let me make it up to you."

"I think I could do that. What did you have in mind?"

"I'd like to take you out on a date. Now granted, it won't be anything spectacular, but I was thinking lunch here in the gardens?"

He's tentative, almost shy. I do recognize that this is a big step and one that I think we were both holding out on until Rebecca knew about us. Maybe it's time to take the next step, now that she knows.

"I'd like that. I can make lunch for us."

"Nope, you let me handle all the planning. All you need to do is show up. Tomorrow?"

"Tomorrow works for me."

"Now, tell me how your meeting with Rebecca went. I know we have lunch with her in a few days. Her husband will be there too, right?"

"Yes, Dale will be there. She was shocked when I told her, but she seemed happy for us. Of course, she wanted to follow me back here that night to check on you, and I was able to at least put that off."

We're quiet for a moment, but Levi keeps looking over at me, studying me closely.

"There's something you aren't telling me."

"I don't know if I should be thrilled that you can read me so well or be scared of it. But it's not anything that I'm hiding. I'm very uneasy about this lunch. Rebecca may be my best friend, but how would you feel about having lunch with my ex-boyfriend?"

His entire body tenses up next to me, and we stop walking near the small waterfall. As I wait for him to speak, the sound of the trickling water is comforting.

"I wouldn't agree to have a double date with your ex-boyfriend. I'd say they're an ex for a reason and I don't see why they need to be in our life. So, I see where you're coming from, but this situation is different. I'm not looking at this as lunch with my ex-girlfriend so much as I'm looking at it as lunch with your best friend."

Taking a minute, I make my mind shift that this is lunch with my best friend. If I look at it that I'm going to be introducing him to my best friend and ignoring the fact that he knows her, well, that makes it a little easier.

Finally, I'm able to put all the worry of the lunch away and focus on Levi. I know he's been walking the garden with me, but it hits me that we walked to the back of the garden, and this is the furthest I've seen him walk.

"How are you feeling? I just realized how far we actually walked! How are you doing?"

A proud smile covers his face.

"Well, I'm not running any marathons, but I'm doing fine walking. Vince has me walking several miles a day on the treadmill with the prosthetic. I'm comfortable enough with it that I'm wearing it all day, though I'm not up and moving as much as I'd like just yet."

"And how steady are you with it?"

He stops and turns to face me with a smirk on his face.

"It depends on what I'm doing."

"What if you were kissing me?"

He doesn't speak again to answer, instead, he leans forward and shows me. His lips land on mine and I gently place my arms on his shoulders, more to have a place to rest them, and he smiles against my lips.

"Wrap your arms around me. Don't you dare hold back," he whispers against my lips before kissing me again.

Then I'm wrapping my arms around him, pulling him close and kissing him with everything I have, until Ace decides we've had enough and starts barking.

We pull away laughing, and head back inside.

"Don't forget lunch tomorrow. I'll come to get you at noon." He says when we reach his room.

"There is no way I'm forgetting our date." I place a soft kiss on his lips.

# Chapter 20

## Levi

Today is my date with Mandy and I've spent all morning making sure every detail is right. I would love nothing more than to be able to take her out on a real date, pick her up at her door, and totally spoil her, but my options are limited right now.

I employed Lexi's help in setting up a picnic. So that we won't be disturbed and wanting a place that was out of the way, Lexi let me use the garden area behind her house.

When Lexi pokes her head in, I've just finished getting dressed. "Everything is all set up. The food is in the cooler, and I've made sure that you will be alone," she says with a huge smile on her face.

Trying to hide my nerves, I turn to face her, "Thank you for this."

"Mandy is a friend, and I'm always happy to help. Plus, it's fun being in on it. Just take a deep breath and make sure you enjoy it. Even though you're nervous, that's to be expected. But have fun, relax, so she can, and then enjoy it because you only get a first date with someone once."

Isn't that the truth? If this goes all wrong, I could really screw everything up with us, and we've come so far to let that happen. I look over my clothes one more time. Even though I know it's a warm day, I'll be wearing long pants because I'm still not at the point where I want to show off my prosthetic leg to the world, much less to Mandy.

Ace has been sitting and watching me get ready this whole time, and I can only imagine what he's thinking.

"You ready to go outside and play, boy?" He's smart and has picked up on some words and knows what outside means, so he gets up and dances in circles by the door until I get there.

Once we step out into the hallway, he's calm, relaxed, and walks by my side, and is very alert to his surroundings. He doesn't like people getting too close to me, but he isn't aggressive about it either. It's like he knows to keep a boundary around me so nothing can potentially cause me to lose my balance.

We take the elevator down to Mandy's office. Before I can knock on the door frame to let her know that we're here, she spots us.

"Right on the time. I was just closing everything on my computer." She finishes up and then stands, walking over to me. She's in a stunning dark green maxi dress with some cute little wedge sandals.

When she's finally standing right in front of me, instead of greeting me, she turns her attention to Ace. He gets all the attention lately, and he eats it right up. Can't blame the dog. If a pretty woman was giving me that much attention, I'd enjoy every minute of it, too.

Almost like she can hear my thoughts, Mandy straightens and looks at me with a soft smile. I lean in, giving her a chaste kiss, hoping to relieve some of the tension, before taking her hand and leading her outside.

On the walk over to Lexi and Noah's house, I catch Mandy looking over at me and grinning. When I catch her the fourth time, I have to know why.

"Why are you looking at me like that?"

"I'm just thinking about how far you've come, and I bet you don't even realize it. Seriously, I'm not just talking about going from being in a wheelchair and now walking. When I met you, it seemed like you had the world on your shoulders, and you refused to share it with anyone. Now you just seem lighter."

I feel lighter and I'm not sure why, though I think it has to do with her by my side, which has changed everything for me. When I don't think I have it in me to push anymore, simply thinking of her gives me that reason. But the topic is a little too heavy for what I'd like to talk about on our date tonight.

I lead her over to the blanket spread on the ground, and her eyes go wide. Then she kisses my cheek before she sits down.

"Would you believe I've never been on a real picnic?" I go to sit down and realize I didn't think this whole thing out with my leg and being a little unsteady.

Sitting down will be easy, but it's standing back up that I'm worried about. Then, seeing how happy she is, and letting what she just said sink in, I realize that I could worry about that part of it later.

"My mom took us out for picnics to kick off spring and then again in the fall. Usually a couple of times a year. It was her way of having a little free time with us when my dad was too busy."

"When I was at school, I'd like to eat my lunch outside mostly because it was the only time I got to spend outdoors. Then when I would get back to whatever foster home I was living at the time, I would hide out in my room, and try to be seen as little as possible. All of that changed when I started hanging out with Rebecca."

I pull out the sandwiches that Lexi had made for us, along with the homemade potato chips, and fudge brownies for dessert.

"You totally just gave yourself away. I know you had help because I would recognize Lexi's fudge brownies a mile away," Mandy laughs.

"She totally set all this up here so that we wouldn't be disturbed."

After we take the first couple bites of our sandwiches, we're silent. But it's a comfortable one, the kind that you can only have when you're truly at ease around someone.

"Ace seems to be having a ball." She nods behind us where Ace is running around chasing some butterflies in the yard.

"He gets along with anybody and anything anywhere that he goes. But he really likes going with me to PT because when I'm on a treadmill Vince will put him on a treadmill right beside me and he thinks it's just the greatest thing ever. I laugh because everybody gets a kick out of it."

"That's pretty amazing. How's PT going?"

"It's going well. Actually, Vince is getting ready to begin teaching me how to drive again. He thinks I'm ready. And I am ready, and excited too."

"Levi, that's great!" she places her hand on mine, and I interlace our fingers for just a moment before we both take our hands back to continue eating our sandwiches.

"But I don't think I'll be able to drive a stick shift again, though that's a small price to pay to be able to drive again at all. Once I'm cleared to drive, I'd really like to take you out for a more formal date, to treat you how you should be pampered and spoiled on a date."

"You don't know how perfect this is for me. I don't need a fancy restaurant or some big gesture, just something like this, relaxing and getting to talk to you is my idea of a perfect date. The only exception to that is going out to get ice cream." Smiling, her big honey-colored eyes light up, and I want to kiss her again. She just has a way of putting me at ease.

While we finish eating, the conversation flows easily, and you'd never know that this was our first date. But truly, we're really past that stage in our relationship.

We sit and talk long after we finish eating, and eventually, Ace comes and lies down next to us and falls asleep without a care in the world. At one point, there is a lull in the conversation, and she tilts her head up to the sun. It catches the highlights in her dirty blonde hair, and she looks so beautiful. She radiates peace and has a Mona Lisa like smile on her face. When her eyes meet mine again, I can't not kiss her.

Like a moth drawn to a flame, I'm pulled into her, and my lips are on hers before I even have time to stop and think. When she lifts a hand to my hair, we slowly lay down with her still kissing me. Not once do our lips leave each other.

The sensation of her hands running through my hair, and her lips on mine overwhelm my system. It's been so long since anyone had touched me, much less touched me like this.

As her hands slide down my neck and over my shoulders to my chest, I freeze. Of course, she picks up on it. Pulling away, she looks into my eyes. "What's wrong?" Her voice barely above a whisper.

Well, what is wrong? To be able to tell her I'd have to know myself, and I'm not sure I even know. While I love her touching me, and her hands on my body, I know that isn't it. I don't mind the few scars on my chest and stomach.

Since I can't put my finger on what's wrong, I decide to stay as close to the truth as possible.

"I'm just not ready for more than this," I say, waiting for a reaction.

Her hand leaves my chest and comes back up to brush some hair from my face before she offers me a soft smile. Her eyes run over my face, and I feel them as if her hand was caressing every inch.

"It's okay. I don't want to screw this up. So I'm all right with us moving slowly. We can even watch snails pass by us."

Relief washes over me. Then she lies down on the blanket next to me, and we both stare up at the sky. When I pull her into my side, she rests her head on my shoulder. I try to soak up this perfect day, and not think about the lunch ahead with Rebecca.

# Chapter 21

## Mandy

My bedroom is a disaster. I think I've tried on every outfit I own at least twice. To say this lunch with Rebecca and her husband is making me nervous is an understatement.

Thankfully, it's my day off of work, so I have a little extra time to get ready, but Rebecca texted me that they were on their way about half an hour ago, which means I need to get moving. After sending three possible outfit ideas to Lexi, she picked out the leggings, oversized sweater, and ankle boots.

Since it's colder today, and I trust her fashion advice, I decide to go with her pick. Finishing my hair and makeup, I give myself one last look in the mirror and decide that this is as good as it's going to get. I grab my keys, phone, and purse and head out the door.

On the way to Oakside, I try to crank up my radio, and not let my mind wander, but it's no use. There are a million different ways that this lunch could go. One direction is Rebecca could be completely fine with it, but Dale isn't. Or Rebecca could come in and decide that she isn't okay with all this, and then I have no idea where that would put everything.

If this lunch doesn't go well, I could be losing my best friend, I could lose Levi, or I could lose both. Lexi has already promised to be in and out of the dining room in case I need rescuing. Paisley promised the same, so I have a couple of people looking out for me, which makes me feel better. They also said I could send them an SOS text if needed.

I just keep reminding myself that this lunch is on my territory, and I've got people that have my back. Besides, it's in public, so how bad can it really get?

Pulling up to Oakside, my first stop is my office, where I hide my purse in the file cabinet. It's more out of habit than anything else, but I really don't want to carry my purse around, and I don't want to leave it in the car either. At least that's what I tell myself because, in reality, I'm just stalling in my safe space.

Glancing at the clock, I realize I can't put this off anymore, so I go upstairs to Levi's room. He's standing by his dresser, looking off into space, as he rolls up the sleeves of his button-down shirt.

"It's such a simple move, yet you make it look so sexy," I smirk as I lean against the doorway.

When he turns to face me, he has a playful smile on his face.

"And what move would that be?"

"Just standing there casually rolling up your sleeves."

He laughs, but it's not the full carefree laugh that I got to witness on our picnic date the other day. I guess we're both nervous, and we're just going to have to support each other through this lunch.

Taking his hand, we head out, stopping in the courtyard to let Ace run around for a minute and do his business before walking into the lobby.

When we sit on the couch, it's as if Ace understands what's happening today because he climbs up and sits between us, putting just enough space that we both calm down and relax.

It's peaceful in the lobby as we both watch the door as well as the other people moving in and out. Zoning out a little as I stare out the window, I can hear Levi talk to one of the other patients.

I don't know how long I'm daydreaming, but I don't see Rebecca and Dale until they're standing almost right in front of us. Levi wraps up his conversation, and we both stand, greeting them.

Even though the greeting is a little awkward, Rebecca hugs me, and Dale shakes Levi's hand. Then we switch and Dale gives me a side hug while Rebecca gives Levi a full-on hug, a much bigger one than she even gave me. To say that it makes things uncomfortable is an understatement.

A glance up at Dale confirms this. The look on his face as he stares at Rebecca and Levi says he's feeling about the same way I am about this. When Rebecca finally pulls back, Levi looks uncomfortable as he glances at me. But I don't even offer him a smile because I really can't. Yet Rebecca doesn't seem to pick up on any of this.

"So, who's this guy?" Rebecca leans down to pet Ace, who doesn't look too sure that he wants her in his space but is being polite, anyway.

"This is Ace. He was one of the MP dogs that were stationed with me overseas," Levi says leaving out a lot of the information.

"Oh, that's great that they assigned you a dog. I bet that made deployments easier," Rebecca says.

"He wasn't assigned to me."

"Oh well, still it's great that he's with you now," Rebecca is so not reading between the lines.

Levi begins to look uncomfortable, and I know this is not a subject he wants to talk to her about. Thankfully, Dale seems to pick up on it. He wraps an arm around his wife's waist and leans close to her ear, whispering something. When her eyes go wide, I know she finally understands what Levi wasn't wanting to say out loud.

She doesn't say anything else, but pets Ace, who puts up with it for just a moment before standing up and walking over to my side as if he's trying to get away from her. She studies Ace for a moment before she stands up.

"So can we have a bit of a tour before we eat?" she asks, her bubbly personality back in place.

"She was eating in the car, and made me stop for some boiled peanuts she'd been craving and that she had to have. But give her about twenty minutes and she'll be starving again," Dale says with a forced smile.

"This little one is going to be a foodie just like his mama. We love to eat."

Giving Rebecca and Dale the shortened tour, we show them the wing that has the dining room, the library, the PT room, and the public courtyard. We end the tour on the back porch where they can see the new barn.

"Can I see your room?" Rebecca asks.

While I know we aren't in high school anymore, but that was a line that she would use to get a guy alone. She used it even more in college and something about her asking Levi just sits wrong with me. But I don't feel like I have the authority to say no, so I turn my back on the group and look out over the side of the porch.

Ace joins me, jumping up and resting his two front paws on the porch railing. He stands there almost like he's a human looking out over the yard and taking it all in. Then I give a small chuckle, wrapping my arm around him and pet him as he stands there by me.

The problem is this side of the porch looks to the tree line, and on the other side of the tree line is Lexi and Noah's property, where we had our picnic date just a few days ago. I think maybe I missed Levi nodding and then heading inside because it's quiet for a little while before Rebecca speaks again.

"Come on, Mandy is always talking about how these places are set up like a bed-and-breakfast, and I want to see," she says in an almost flirty tone.

"No," Levi growls, but a moment later he's at my side with his arm around my waist.

I still can't bring myself to look at him, because I knew that this lunch was going to go bad, and this is just an omen that this is just the beginning. But if I were to say anything, I would be crazy and judgmental, so I bite my tongue and try to force a smile as I turn to face Rebecca and Dale.

"Let's go grab some lunch," Levi says, leaving no room for a change in subject.

Ace and I lead the way into the dining room as Rebecca walks with Levi and Dale trails behind all of us. We get in line and get our food, including a small little treat for Ace, before taking a seat by one of the windows towards the back of the room.

Levi and Rebecca sit across from each other, and I take my seat next to Levi and Dale sits next to Rebecca, across from me. Ace takes his spot under the table, lying on top of my feet facing Levi.

"So, fill me in on what happened. The last thing I knew, you were on your way to boot camp," Rebecca says as we dig into our lunch.

Levi goes on and shares some stories from boot camp and his basic training, all of which I haven't even heard before. He talks about some of the people in his unit and even about his first deployment, but he's staying clear of anything that gets too close to his injury.

"So, what did you do for your twenty-first birthday? You were always saying that you were going to take the guys, go to Vegas, and get stupid drunk," Rebecca says.

"I was deployed on my birthday, so I wasn't able to celebrate until I got back stateside, then all the guys took me out to go bar hopping."

Just like that, Rebecca is bringing up old memory after old memory of high school, plans they had made when they were together to see if he kept up on them. She shares about her college days but always circles back around to the two of them in high school.

Just like I used to when I hung out with them in high school, I feel completely like a third wheel. Looking at Dale, I can tell that he's not amused by any of this. Dale has always been easy-going, levelheaded, and head over heels in love with Rebecca. But right now, all I see is anger and irritation on his face, and that's not something I've ever seen before.

Ace is able to pick up on the atmosphere and the more uncomfortable I get, the more he starts shifting around and rubbing his head on my leg. Levi has completely forgotten that I'm here, and so has Rebecca, exactly like when I would tag along in high school.

Suddenly, I feel like that girl all over again. The girl that didn't have a lot of friends, so I would deal with being the third wheel just to be out of the house. The girl who didn't have a family to go to didn't have anybody else and was just trying to stay out of the way.

In the back of my head, I know I'm not that girl anymore and I've come a long way. I have friends that care about me, and while I still don't have a family like them, but I feel like Lexi and Noah have become my family.

Speaking of which, I decide that I'd had enough, and pull out my phone.

**Me:** SOS
**Lexi:** I'm on my way. Sorry it sucked.
**Me:** Tell you all about it.

A minute later, Lexi is walking into the room, and relief fills me. She looks around the room and when she spots us, she beelines over.

"I'm sorry to interrupt. Mandy, I know this is your day off, but we have an issue with one of the donors that we need your help with. It should only be a minute or two," Lexi says.

I force a smile for Dale, who I'm sure knows exactly what's going on, even though Levi and Rebecca barely give me enough attention to realize that I'm leaving.

"I'll take Ace with me since he's been fidgeting. I think he has to go outside, but I'll bring him back in a little bit," I say, and finally, Levi looks at me, giving me a small nod, and turns back to Rebecca.

Ace follows me as I go with Lexi downstairs to her office. I close the door as Lexi digs out some doggy treats that she keeps on her desk. Ace gladly takes one and goes to lie in the corner of the room.

"It was like I wasn't even there. Not once did they include me in the conversation over lunch. It was just Rebecca going on and on about memory after memory of high school, and did he do this, or did he do that like he had planned. What did you do for your twenty-first birthday? Did you go out to Vegas as you had always said you were going to?" I grumble as I collapse on the couch beside Lexi.

"Well, they haven't seen each other in years, so I'm sure it's great to take a walk down memory lane," Lexi says, but even I don't believe her.

"We were in high school all over again, and I was the third wheel, who was just hanging around, so I didn't have to go home. And poor Dale, he actually looked angry, and I've never seen him mad; he's always so easygoing."

Lexi pulls me in for a hug and then turns the TV in her office on, and we get lost in a couple of home improvement shows for the next hour.

"Well, I've avoided them long enough. He should be back in his room, and I guess I should go take Ace to him."

At the mention of his name, Ace pops his head up and looks at me. He'd been napping this whole time, content to just relax, and can't say I blame him.

"I know this isn't the ideal time to ask, but I have a doctor's appointment. It's our first one with the doctor that we really like, and they had a cancellation. They were able to get us in a little earlier tomorrow. Would you be willing to watch over the place until we get in later in the afternoon?" Lexi asks.

"Of course, I'd love to."

"We'll be getting a room ready for a new patient, and I'll leave all the details and his file on your desk so that you have it if they show up early."

Then I stand and give Lexi another hug, wanting to avoid going up and seeing Levi altogether.

When I get up to Levi's room, I find him staring out the window. Even though I stopped in the doorway, Ace runs right to his side getting his attention. Instantly, I realize that I don't want to talk about this right now. I just want to go home. I feel emotionally drained and would do anything for a nap, so when Levi turns and finally looks at me, I speak first.

"Wanted to bring him back to you, but I've got to get going." I turn and start to walk down the hallway.

"Mandy."

I don't even stop as I take the stairs down to my office, grab my stuff, and get out to my car and off the property as soon as I can. By the time I get home and collapse on my bed, I can't decide if I want to cry or yell.

Either way, I turn my phone off, turn the TV on, and let the tears come. Though I'm not sure if they're sad or angry ones.

# Chapter 22

"Hi, I'm Lauren." The bubbly girl in front of me says like I'm supposed to know who she is.

I'm standing at the front desk at Oakside, but I've been so zoned out thinking of the lunch yesterday that I've gotten next to nothing done. Lexi and Noah are at their doctor's appointment, where they're finding out if it's a boy or a girl. Then I told Noah to take her out to lunch after.

Shaking my head, I focus on the woman in front of me. "Sorry, I was a million miles away. Who are you?"

She studies me for a minute before placing a hand on my arm.

"Are you okay? You look like there's something pretty heavy on your mind?"

"There is, but this is not the time or place to talk about it," I tell her honestly.

"I'll respect that. I'm sorry. I know I'm prying but it's my nature to get people to open up to me. Lexi hired me. There's a new patient coming in who is blind, and I'm here to adapt his room for him. Now that he has no sight, I'll be working with him to get him to function on his own."

"Oh yes! I did look at the folder Lexi left me. Listen, I'm sorry. This is not my best day." I take a furtive look down the hallway where Levi's room is. It's on the same floor where we are setting up the room for the new patient.

Today I stalked Levi's schedule to make sure I was able to avoid him as much as possible, and I'm not ashamed to admit it. Right now he's in PT, so there's no chance of running into him in the hallway.

"Follow me. I will show you the room," I say, heading down the hallway.

As we pass Levi's room, I tense up, but thankfully find it empty, so I continue down to the end of the hallway. Finally arriving at what I call the blue room. There is a beautiful blue accent wall behind the bed, hardwood floors, leather chairs, and a sofa. A wood desk in the corner with a matching dresser has a TV on it. As with every room here, it has its own private bathroom.

"This is the room Lexi picked out," I say as we step in.

Lauren looks around the room without saying anything and then walks around taking everything in before looking back at me.

"I can work with this. But we need to remove a few things, like the rug and some of these miscellaneous pieces, until he learns his way around. Then we can add them back."

"Make a list of what needs to be taken away or anything that you'd like added, and we will take care of it. Since we still have a few more weeks before the hospital will be ready to release him, we can make sure that the room is ready to go." I say, remembering what I read in the file.

"This is my first time working with Oakside, and I have to say these rooms are nicer than my own bedroom. It's wonderful to see your facility wanting to spoil the veterans instead of making them feel like they're still locked in a hospital," she says, glancing around the room.

"Lexi and Noah started this place because there wasn't any place like it when Noah got out of the hospital. Lexi's biggest want was that it didn't feel like a hospital, but for it to feel more like a bed-and-breakfast."

"Well, she definitely achieved it."

"And each room is different. They wanted the men and women here to feel like they had their own room and not just a cookie-cutter room." I go on to tell her a bit about the different rooms, and how Lexi kept the history of the building as much as possible in them.

"Come on. Let me show you around the grounds." Taking her to the courtyard and then out to the back porch, I conveniently avoid Levi as he's getting ready to get out of his appointment and go back to his room.

Almost like Paisley knows I need an excuse to hang out on the back porch, she and Easton are both there with their dogs and chat with Lauren for a while.

Though Lauren is nice and friendly, she appears more interested in playing and learning about the dogs. Apparently, she works with training seeing-eye dogs for soldiers, and she and Paisley hit it off right away. Already, they are making plans to meet for lunch later this week.

The entire time, Easton stands there and watches over Paisley with a smile on his face. Though he's not a huge fan of new people, and I know with his history of being a prisoner of war that some situations are difficult for him still. But he's come a long way, and the love that is on his face as he watches Paisley make friends is evident to everyone.

He's happy to stand back and watch her be the center of attention. All the while watching over her and having her back completely. We can all hope to find someone like that one day.

Finally, we say our goodbyes and go back into the lobby.

"Everyone I've met here is really nice, and it seems like a fun place to work," Lauren says.

"Easton is a former patient here, and he's now our head of security. I had a front-row seat of watching those two fall in love and seeing Easton finally come out of his shell. To be honest, watching any of these patients overcome their injuries, stand up on their feet again, and take their life back is amazing to watch."

Then I proceed to show her where the dining room is, and that's where my luck runs out. Levi is there, and he spots us, waving me over to where he's sitting.

"Give me just a minute and then I'll show you the rest of this wing."

"Oh, take your time." She gestures to me that she'll wait.

I hesitantly walk over to Levi, not wanting to start a commotion in the middle of the dining room.

"Can we talk?" he asks when I walk up to the table.

"No. Lexi left me in charge of the place today because she has a doctor's appointment, and I'm showing someone around who is helping get a room ready for an incoming patient. I don't have time to sit down and talk."

Though I try to keep my emotions out of it, even to my ears, I sound a little robotic. Knowing that any emotion on his face would make my resolve crumble, I don't even look at him.

"Can we talk later?" he asks in a hopeful voice.

"I don't know, but I've got to go." With that, I turn and go to Lauren, trying to force a smile on my face. Wrapping up the tour, I take her to the library, and then show her the PT room.

"Well, I'm going to go inventory his room and make that list," she says once the tour is over.

"When you're done, I'll be at the front desk. Come find me, and I will make sure Lexi and Noah get the list."

We say our goodbyes, and she goes to the room as I head up to the front desk. My mind starts racing with what to say to Levi, knowing that he's going to pass me leaving the dining room on the way back to his room. When he finds me alone, this time he's not going to drop the issue.

About twenty minutes later, just as I suspected, Levi finds me at the front desk, and there's nothing for me to distract myself.

"Who was that you were with earlier?" he asks.

"Her name is Lauren. She's a specialist that they are bringing in to help a new patient who has lost his sight."

"Please talk to me, Mandy. I know something is wrong, but I can't fix it if I don't know what it is."

"There was no budget emergency yesterday. I sent Lexi an SOS text because the lunch was horrible." I come clean.

He keeps his emotions in check as he studies my face, but I have to look away.

"Why was it so horrible?" he asks.

I shake my head in disbelief that he doesn't understand what happened.

"You and Rebecca dominated that conversation. Dale and I didn't say a single word. You two took a trip down memory lane, and Rebecca was completely fine with rubbing it in how well she knew what your plans were and how well she knew you. In all honesty, it felt like I was back in high school. All those times I hung out with the two of you so that I didn't have to go home, and you didn't include me. I know Dale felt the same way, and that's his wife, so I can only imagine the conversation that they had, which means that it's going to be even worse the next time I talk to her."

"You know I wouldn't want to make you feel that way. But it was nice to talk to someone who shared some of the same memories, but I never meant to make you feel like a third wheel."

"What you really mean is it was good to take a trip down memory lane with Rebecca. But I was there in high school, and at the same parties. Every party you two were at, so was I. But it's like you guys forgot that I was ever part of your little friend group, which is fine because it shows me exactly where I stand."

My eyes start to sting with the telltale sign that I'm about to cry, and I once again don't know if it's because I'm upset or just angry at myself.

"It was never my intention to make you feel that way and I'm sorry that I did." He says, trying to take my hand, but I pull away.

"The thing is, I know Rebecca, and she knew exactly what she was doing. This means she's not as okay with this as she thought she was, and it was her way of showing me that you were hers. Even though she's married, I still can't compete with her, and I don't want to. So, I think that we need to slow things down."

As I say it, it's the last thing I want, and my heart breaks. Really I don't want us to slow things down or let him go, but it's my responsibility to stick by my friend too. Rebecca is the one person that has been in my life the longest and has been there for me. Without a doubt, I know I handled this all wrong, hell it never should have even started.

Rebecca had always been there for me growing up. When everyone at school avoided 'the foster care kid', she walked right up to me and made me her best friend. She made sure I experienced high school, the dances, football games, and prom.

Even if it meant letting me raid her closet to do it, she made sure I had the whole experience. She wouldn't go to a party if I couldn't go. If certain people wouldn't hang out with me, then she wouldn't hang out with them, no matter how much I told her it was okay, she didn't waver.

Someone having my back like that means more than I can even express. I need to make sure I make things right with her because she wouldn't ever do anything like this to me.

"The last thing I want is any distance between us or to take it any slower," Levi says. "But if that's what you want, and if that's what you need, then I'll give it to you. But I'm not walking away, and we're not done."

My heart soars that he wants our relationship to continue and wants to spend time with me. Even though he isn't dropping this, at the same time I wish he would, because maybe it would make everything easier all around.

Trying to end this conversation, I say, "I have more work to do before Lexi gets back."

Levi stands there and stares at me for a minute, but all I want is space, to be able to head downstairs for a few minutes and get my emotions in check without someone watching me.

"You take some time, but I'm telling you, Mandy, this isn't over. We are not over, and I will make this up to you."

I know it's not, and that's what scares me.

# Chapter 23

## Levi

It's been a week since Mandy and I had our argument over the disastrous lunch with Rebecca and her husband.

Each day that passes, Mandy seems to be getting better and is opening up to me. In retrospect, I guess I should have gone with my gut instinct and not had the lunch at all.

It was great to reconnect with Rebecca, but not at the expense of hurting Mandy. I won't make that mistake again.

Today has been back-to-back appointments. From my PT appointment to meeting with some counselors and therapists, they all seem to fall today of all days. By the time I make it back to my room, I'm stressed, and to be honest, Oakside is the last place I really want to be.

Trying to de-stress, I turn on the TV to relax, and about half an hour later, in walks

Mandy. She looks just as irritated as I am. Then she leans against the doorframe, not even stepping into my room before looking at me.

"I hope your day was better than mine," she says.

"Not very likely," I tell her.

She looks over at the TV and then back over at me.

"You want to get out of here for a bit?"

"Out of my room or out of Oakside?" I ask hopefully.

"Out of Oakside. I've got one of my meatloaves in the freezer. At my house, I can warm them up, have better TV than you have got here, and of course, Ace is welcome. There's even a yard for him to run around in."

You don't have to tell me twice. I'm already standing up and turning the TV off before I answer her. "Even if it's only for an hour, I want nothing more than to get out of here."

Following her out to the lobby where she signs me out, we then go out to her car. I guess that's one advantage to being up and walking again, that I can leave if someone's willing to take me.

This will be my first time out of Oakside since I came here. As grateful as I am for this place, I need a break for sure.

The car ride is short, and as we pull up to the small cottage home surrounded by large oak trees, my nerves start to set in. This is a big step in our relationship, being truly alone and out of Oakside.

Ace seems to have no problem being here. He jumps out of the car and starts running around the front yard, sniffing everything. Leaning against the car, I stand and watch him. He loves being outside, and I know I need to let him run more, even if it's just in the courtyard.

"If you want to stay out here and play with him, you can. But the backyard is fenced, and I have a doggie door which he may or may not know how to use."

"Ace, come on boy," I call him and follow Mandy into the house.

Despite how small it looks on the outside, the light wall colors and bright furniture make the space feel much larger. Her living room has a couch and a recliner. Once Ace spots the recliner, he beelines for it and sits in it like he is a king on a throne.

Before I even get to worry about him being on her furniture, Mandy laughs at him.

"You are just going to stake a claim, huh? Well, be warned. You will have to fight Noah for that chair when he visits." She says, petting him. He cocks his head to the side as if to say, 'and you think he will win?'

I follow Mandy into the kitchen which is just as light and bright as the living room.

"Let me put the meatloaf in and we can watch some TV. I hope you don't mind instant mashed potatoes, as I just don't have the energy to deal with making the real ones tonight."

"Instant mashed potatoes are still a giant improvement to the ones they served when we were overseas," I say, smirking.

"Well, then I guess I should be honest and say that the biscuits will also be from a can and not homemade. But the meatloaf I made and then froze."

"Honestly, I wouldn't care if we were having TV dinners. It's just nice to get out of there for a while." I tell her, watching her set the oven.

When she turns back to me, she takes my hand and leads me to the couch. Ace has settled in the recliner and laid down with his head on the arm of the chair, so he has the perfect view of the TV with his good eye.

Finally settling on the couch, we easily agree on a funny movie to watch. When she snuggles into my side, I wrap my arm around her, and it's just easy being here with her like this. As she laughs at different parts of the movie and her body shakes against mine, all I can think about is how nice it would be if this was my reality every day.

If I want this to be every day, to make that happen, I still have a lot of work to do. Almost like she can read my mind, Mandy looks up at me with a smile on her face that reaches her eyes.

Not wanting to talk and ruin the moment, I simply lean in and kiss her. But I can't get her close enough, and instinctively she straddles my lap and presses her chest to mine. When she settles right on my hard cock, I groan.

"This, okay?" She whispers in concern.

"Fuck, it's more than okay," I say and then recapture her lips with mine and pull her hips down on me again.

Hesitantly, she grinds on my erection, causing us both to moan and making me want more. Before we get the chance to take things any further, the timer in the kitchen goes off.

"Damn." She says, pulling back.

"To be continued," I tell her, gripping her hips and not letting her move until she nods her head.

As she heads into the kitchen, I take a few deep breaths, getting myself under control. After a few minutes, I follow her into the kitchen, and Ace follows me. When he sees the doggy door, he sniffs around it before putting his head through and looking out into the backyard.

Then he pulls his head back in, sitting by the door and looking at me like he's waiting for permission to go outside. I give him a good scratch behind his ears because I couldn't have gotten any luckier with a better-trained dog.

"You can go outside, buddy. Go play," I say, nodding my head toward the doggie door.

Ace hesitantly turns back to the doggy door and slowly works his way through it, but once outside, he starts running around again, smelling every part of the yard.

As she finishes up dinner, I help Mandy set the table. When we sit down, Ace comes in checking for food and then goes back out to run, chasing whatever he finds in the yard. By the time we finished dinner, he's lying on the back porch watching us through the large sliding glass doors.

"I think he's claimed this as his home, so you might have a hard time getting rid of him now." I joke with Mandy as we clean off the table.

"I have no reason to want to get rid of him or you," she shrugs.

When she starts to clean the dishes, I stop her.

"The dishes can wait. Let's go watch some more TV and relax." Without a doubt, I'm sure she can read between the lines that, more than anything, I want to continue what we started before dinner.

Since I have no intention of watching it, I agree with the first movie she suggests. Once she gets the movie going, it seems she doesn't either because we don't even get past the opening credits before she's cuddled up to me, and her lips are on mine.

Without wasting any time, I pull her onto my lap, and she comes willingly. Even over our clothes, when she begins grinding on me, the motion feels amazing. Especially when it's been so long since anyone but myself had touched my cock.

"How far we take this is up to you. Just say the word," I tell her, wanting her to know she's in control.

"What if I want to go all the way?" She then starts kissing my neck, and her lips move downward toward places I would like her to go.

Holding back a moan, I grit out, "I'd ask why you still had your pants on."

Standing, she immediately starts undressing. I whip off my shirt, and it seems to distract her because she stops what she's doing and leans forward to smooth her hands over my arms and then my abs.

"You still have on too many clothes," I smirk as she starts undressing again.

Hesitating on the zipper to my pants, because I don't want to remove them and have her see my leg. But she is going to expect me to get undressed too. Reading my mind and sensing the war going on in my head, she drops to her knees in front of me.

"Trust me. We don't have to remove your pants all the way. Only what you are comfortable with." She unbuttons my pants and helps me pull them down enough that my cock springs free.

When she slowly begins pulling my pants down another inch, I stop her. She doesn't hesitate to climb back into my lap. Even though she doesn't know she gave me a great gift right now, I'll focus on that later. Right now, all I want to do is make this girl cum over and over again.

When her wet core slides along my cock, I'm about to lose it. She is soaking wet already, making me glad I wasn't the only one affected by all the teasing before dinner. I stop her movements for a moment because I want to be able to take her body in.

Her cheeks flush red under my gaze, and her nipples tighten to stiff points. My lips are drawn to them like a magnet. Then I suck one of her delectable nipples into my mouth, getting my first taste of her body. Instantly I'm addicted. My dick gets even harder than I ever thought possible. She must feel it because she tries to move again. But I hold her still.

"You are so damn beautiful," I murmur before moving to the other nipple.

It's been so long since I've been with anyone that this will probably be over embarrassingly fast. But I want to make sure she cums, so I rub her clit with my thumb. When her whole body jolts like it's been shocked, she falls forward and collapses on me.

I kiss her as I gently thrust two fingers into her. Her silky warm channel grips me tight as she moans. She's already so close that I slow down to draw out her orgasm. With every thrust and every movement, I'm learning her body. She is so responsive, my cock is begging to join the party.

When I increase my pace and put pressure on her clit, she falls apart for me. Mandy letting go this way for me is a heady feeling. Having her trust me like this is an honor I don't take lightly.

As her body starts to relax, I remove my fingers and lick her juices off. They're musky and sweet, and I'm afraid I'm hooked on her, addicted to her scent, to her body.

"Your turn," she smiles, moving to climb off my lap. I stop her.

"No baby, I'm barely hanging on," I tell her, and she gets my message and settles herself back in my lap.

Resting her hand on my shoulder, her eyes meet mine and all the emotion I'm feeling is reflected in her eyes. I'm about to line my cock up to thrust into her, but then I realize

I'm not wearing a condom. I've never come this close to slipping up.

"I don't have a condom, baby."

"Oh, I do!" She pops up and hurries down the hallway next to the living room, her gorgeous curvy naked body on full display. In no time at all, she's back to me with the foil square in her hand.

Her perfectly round breasts are bouncing with each step, and when she realizes she's naked and uncovered, she gives me a shy smile as her face turns beet red.

"You walking into this room is the sexiest thing I have ever seen," I tell her as I take the condom and roll it on.

She settles back in my lap, and this time when my cock is at her entrance, there is no hesitation from either of us. With one languid move of her hips, she slides down my length causing us both to moan out loud.

It feels like there is a vice in my chest squeezing my heart, and at the same time, nothing has ever felt so damn right. I sense that this is where I was always meant to be. I'm not thinking about my leg, I'm thinking about the gorgeous woman riding my dick and that I need to get her off again because I'm already ready to blow.

"Slow down baby, we aren't in any rush," I grip her hips to set a slow pace.

"You feel so good." She moans, tossing her head back and thrusting her chest into my face.

"Trust me, so do you," I tell her before sucking on her pert plump breasts.

Running my hands up her sides, I fill my hands with them and give them a firm squeeze, which makes her pussy clench around me. She is getting close again, so I reach between us and play with her clit. I don't take it slow, because even at this pace, I'm not going to last much longer.

"Levi, Levi, Levi!" she chants my name and then screams as she falls over the edge, and I finally let go of the orgasm I'd been fighting back. The most intense orgasm I can ever remember having.

As Mandy's body collapses against me, she slides tiny kisses against my neck. Yes, this moment right here is perfect. Too bad I wasn't thinking too far ahead.

• • • • • • • • • •

I start to wake up with Ace licking my face, which means he has to go outside. But when I open my eyes, I realize I'm not in my room back at Oakside. It takes just a moment before all of last night comes crashing back. Looking to my side confirms Mandy is still asleep and lying there.

Eventually, we moved to her room, and I waited until she was asleep last night and removed my prosthetic and my pants. I need to put it back on to be able to take Ace out, but with Mandy laying so peacefully on my arm I don't want to move. As if she can feel my eyes on her, she turns, faces me, and her eyes flutter open.

I tense because as much as I want to be in the moment with her, I know that there's going to be no way of getting my prosthetic back on without her seeing.

"What's wrong?" her brows furrow as she looks at me.

I close my eyes, not answering her because I don't have the words.

"I need to get back to Oakside. I've got a bunch of appointments and I don't want to miss them. Why don't you go get ready, and I will buy breakfast on our way in?"

She leans in, and the moment her lips are on mine, I forget everything and just feel. Her ability to calm me and make me forget whatever is on my mind is something that comforts me, steadies me. That is until her hand starts tracing down my chest toward my hip.

I stop her and grab her hand in mine, pull it up, and place a kiss in the center of her palm.

"Levi, please don't hide from me. Let me see you."

Does she even know what she is asking of me? Letting her see the worst part of me?

"No." I grit out.

"Levi. I don't take what happened last night lightly. Do you?"

I soften. Of course, I don't because last night was a huge step for me too.

"No, I don't," I say, much softer this time.

"Then no secrets between us."

She slowly moves her hand back down to my chest until it gets to the sheet and pulls it down slightly. As soon as she exposes my cock and touches it, I get hard. She gives it a few gentle caresses, making me groan.

As she moves the sheet lower, she never lets up stroking my cock. The sensation of her touching me overpowers the fear of her seeing my stump. Leaning back on the pillow, I focus on how good her hands feel on my cock instead of her looking at my leg.

Then she picks up the pace, leaning down and kissing the scarred skin just below my knee. It surprises me because the sensation is as if she has just put her mouth on my cock. My orgasm hits hard and fast and I cum all over my stomach as I growl out her name.

When I finally come back to myself, I realize what happened, and I look at her and she's looking up at me. It's a sight I will never forget. She kisses the stump again, then crawls up my body and starts licking up the cum off my stomach.

"Fuck, baby." That's all I can say because I'm at a total loss for words.

Of course, it would be this girl to wash away all my anxieties and show me there is nothing to worry about, at least not with her.

# Chapter 24

## Mandy

After walking Levi to his room, I enter my office and I can't wipe the smile off my face. Well, that is, until I see Lexi sitting in my chair with a frown on her face.

"You can't keep him out like that," she says, but her voice is still friendly.

"I hadn't planned on us falling asleep after we had dinner. Ace didn't even wake us up until this morning. By the way, he took over the recliner so he and Noah are going to have to battle it out if they're ever there at the same time."

I pull out my phone and show her a few pictures I took of Ace claiming the chair like a throne, which makes her laugh.

We spend the next half hour talking as friends about what happened last night, and I leave out the details, but I do share that he let me see his leg.

"That is a big step, and it's good because it means he's making progress. Just don't push him too far too fast."

I don't get a chance to speak before Noah walks in holding a piece of mail with a completely dumbfounded and shocked look on his face.

"What's wrong?" Lexi and I both ask at the same time.

He looks up at us for a moment and then back down at the piece of paper in his hands and then back at us with a bewildered look on his face. He opens his mouth to speak a few times and closes it before he's finally able to form words. By then, both Lexi and I are on the edge of our seats.

"You know the band Highway 55?"

We both nod and smile.

"Of course we do! I have a total crush on Dallas," I smile.

"I was always more of a Landon girl myself," Lexi says.

"Too bad they're both married now. And so are you." I give Lexi a disappointed look, but she just shrugs her shoulders and looks back over at her husband. We all know she is head over heels in love with him.

"Well, they just sent us a donation." Noah holds up the letter in his hand.

"That's a good thing, right?" Lexi asks.

"It's a very good thing. The donation is in the amount of five million dollars."

We both gasp and jump up, going to Noah's side to read the letter. What grabs my eye is the check attached with the biggest amount I've ever seen on a donation here, or anywhere for that matter.

Apparently, the band had an issue with their old manager stealing money, so they took him to court, and this five million was what they were awarded.

Since they hadn't really missed the money, they agreed to donate it to charity. Because their bodyguard and now head of security had been a patient here, they decided to donate the money to Oakside.

"Who's the bodyguard that they're talking about?" I ask.

"Mason," Noah says.

"Oh, I really liked Paige. Did they ever get married?"

"Yes, right before he got the job with the band," Lexi says.

"And how have you not gotten concert tickets yet?" I tease her.

She giggles and then we both turn back to the check. This is one of those moments working in a non-profit when you just want to take it in and savor the moment.

"There is so much that we can do with the money. I don't even know where to start," I say in awe.

"Well," Noah says, "I'm going to go to the bank and deposit this check so nothing happens to it. While I'm gone you two make a list of anything that we could spend money on. And I mean anything. Everything that we've talked about, any repairs that need to be made, or the specialist we talked about bringing in. When I get back, we'll go over the list and see if we can't make a game plan."

Noah leaves while Lexi and I are just staring at each other, still in shock.

"I'm going to ask Brooke to watch over this place. Let's head back to my house so we can sit in the sunroom and start planning. I'll have Noah pick us up some lunch from that deli by the bank."

I just nod because I'm still dazed by the check, while Lexi pulls out her phone and starts texting everyone the good news. Going to the golf carts that Noah has been insisting on, we hop on and leave for their house.

Noah finds us in the sunroom with paper scattered all over the coffee table. We've gone over and over, making lists of everything we've ever talked about doing with Oakside. After doing some research, we've added some stuff to the list that wasn't there before.

As the three of us sit down to eat lunch, Noah looks over the list and even adds a few ideas himself. By the time we're done eating, we're ready to dig in and start planning.

You would think with everything that we would like to do at Oakside that deciding how to spend five million would take a lot more time to budget everything out. Yet once we looked at the list, it was very clear how we wanted to spend the money and we had a game plan in just over an hour.

I'm now sitting in my office doing all the formal budgeting to make this happen. We decided to set aside half of it to sponsor some veterans that need help but haven't been able to get their insurance to cover their stay here. Most are suffering from PTSD, and the military has turned its back on them.

After some discussion, we decided to get together next week and figure out how we're going to divvy out that money exactly, so it cuts down my budgeting by half today.

The other half of the money we decided to use to renovate the attic space. It's large enough that we can get four more rooms up there, with a nurse's station, and room for the elevator. There's also the room where the roof starts to slant that we can use for storage.

We already have a rough estimate of how much that's going to cost because we got a bid on it at the beginning of the year. The rest of the money is going towards getting the Aquatic Center up and running.

While we have enough money to build the structure and the Olympic size pool, all of the other details will have to wait, which means this will be the focus of our fundraising for the rest of the year. Noah has big plans for hot tubs, wading pools, water therapy, saunas, and beautiful locker rooms.

He also wants to have an outdoor pool that's more for entertainment and relaxation, not for therapy. That one will have to wait, but just being able to get started on the big pool and the structure alone is putting us a good year or two ahead of schedule.

I'm thinking about making plans for the Aquatic Center as we still have to get some contractors out to give us their bids. After that, we need to start making plans on where the structure is going to be and all of the myriad of details that need to be put in place, which makes my head spin. I'm so lost in budgets, that I don't realize someone is standing in my door until I hear them clearing their throat.

When I look up, I see Rebecca. She offers me a shy smile.

"I'm sorry to bother you at work, but I wanted to talk in person. Do you have a minute?" She says, not moving from the doorway.

"I've been working on the budget for a few hours already. I could use a bit of a break. Why don't you come in?" I stand, moving to my new couch and sit down.

Rebecca closes the door and sits on the opposite end of the couch. he looks nervous and that's never a good sign. I can't imagine this is about anything else other than the lunch that we had the other day. So I'm ready for almost anything.

"I wanted to apologize about the lunch. Dale wasn't very happy with how it went down and made me realize that Lexi was your SOS text to get out of there."

"She was," I say, figuring there's no use in denying the truth at this point.

Rebecca nods and stares at her hands folded in her lap, then she rests one hand on her very pregnant belly before looking back up at me again.

"I guess I didn't realize that I wasn't as okay as I thought I was with you and Levi being together. I thought I was, but it wasn't until I saw you two and the way that he was with you that I realized I was not all right with it."

Hearing her words, I take a deep breath and try to think about what I want to say. Levi and I are in a good place, and I am truly happy. Rebecca has an amazing husband and a child on the way. She has the life that she's always wanted where she doesn't have to work and she's able to help a bunch of charities. Essentially, she gets to be a society wife on a much smaller scale than someone in a big city.

The only difference is Rebecca gets to be one of those truly kind and nice society wives that doesn't have a hidden agenda and is truly there to help the community. She isn't afraid to get her hands dirty by helping someone in need.

I guess that's why I'm a bit shocked at this turn of events. I thought we were all moving past this, but I guess I was wrong. All I know is that there is no going back for me now, not after what Levi and I shared this morning.

"That's something you really could have figured out before my and Levi's relationship progressed this much. But as it stands, you're married, and you really don't have a say in this anymore." I stand and open the door, indicating that I'm done with this conversation.

"I shouldn't have to be okay with this. You are my best friend and under no circumstances should you ever have started dating my ex-boyfriend, no matter what. Then to place me in this type of situation while I'm pregnant and then putting me in a tight spot with my husband. What kind of friend does that?" She raises her voice, causing both Lexi and Noah to come to the door to see what is going on.

Noah steps into my office and away from the doorway, more as a bodyguard in case anything happens. Lexi goes to my side and hooks her arm through mine, showing her support for me.

"You know Rebecca, I've come a long way from that scared girl that would tag along and be the third wheel because she would rather not be at home. I have people that want to hang out with me, who want to be around me, and I'm fine being on my own now as well. You have to know I never set out to hurt you, and I didn't plan this, but with as many memories as you and Levi have, he and I have just as many." I keep my voice flat without emotion.

"Now I think it's time for you to go before you cause a scene, and that is the last thing these soldiers need after everything they've been through," Noah says.

Thankfully, she leaves without causing too much drama, and Noah follows her out to make sure that it stays that way. Me on the other hand, I collapse on the couch, and Lexi sits down beside me, pulling me into a hug without any words.

Of course, it was too good to be true. I've always faded away into the shadows, not wanting to be the center of attention. But the moment that I want something, it's like the universe is working against me saying I don't deserve it.

# Chapter 25

I'm sitting at my desk writing my pen pal **,** when Ace starts stirring, and a moment later, he's really agitated.

"Buddy, what's wrong?" I scratch his head, trying to get him to calm down, and that's when a throat clears in the doorway.

When I turn to see who is there, I'm shocked. Of all the people that could be standing there, I never expected it to be my father. My father looks me over and then turns to Ace as he starts growling at him. He sees Ace's missing eye and shakes his head.

"You managed to find yourself a dog that's as broken as you are," my dad says, staring at Ace.

Why did I expect anything different? No hello. No, how you are doing? Just start everything off with an insult so that I know where he's coming from. But if I learned anything from my time in the military it's how to throw around insults.

"Even missing an eye, he still has better taste than you do," I retort, waiting for my father to continue.

When most people visit Oakside they're dressed in jeans and comfortable clothes. The only people that I've ever seen walking around Oakside in a suit are investors. Somehow my dad walking around in a suit makes him look even more dressed up than the investors have been. But that's my father. He always has to one up everyone.

I guess when I had Noah lift the restrictions on Rebecca visiting, he did it for everyone. Great.

"What are you doing here?" I ask after I finally get tired of the silence and him not speaking.

"As I'm sure you know as your next of kin, we were notified of your injuries and your location," he says not moving from the doorway.

I make a note to change that in my medical records to Mandy or hell, even Noah.

"I am aware. That's why my question wasn't how did you find me, but is what are you doing here."

My dad pauses and looks around the room. You can see almost everything from the doorway.

"It's a nice room here," is all he says.

"Sure, beats the hell out of staying in the hospital." This time I stand, and my father stares at me.

Dropping his eyes, he looks at my legs even though with the pants and shoes on you couldn't tell that one is missing. Under his gaze, I can definitely feel that one is missing.

He finally takes a few steps into my room but remains standing as I take Ace over to the couch. I sit down and Ace gets up on the couch and lies in my lap like he knows I need a buffer between my dad and me. Though I keep petting Ace, trying to get him to calm down, but he's still overly agitated with my dad in the room. I don't blame him because I don't like him here either.

"It's time for you to come home."

"Says who? There's nothing for me there. You know you made sure to remind me of that."

"Your career is over, and you are now useless. What are you going to do with your life? Why don't you just come home and be a drain on the family? At least there, we can contain what the press says about you. Make you not seem so useless with only one leg." To most, my father's voice would sound flat saying that, but I can hear the irritation in it.

His words are a slap to my face. Words that you don't ever want to hear spoken, much less from the man who's supposed to be your father. Ace starts licking my face, sensing that I'm about ready to go off.

"It's okay, buddy," I'm petting him, trying to calm him down.

"I don't give a shit about what makes you look bad. And you couldn't pay me enough money to move back home with you and the family that disowned me. I may not know what my next step is, but it sure as hell has nothing to do with you."

My father doesn't say anything. He just gives me the 'you know you fucked up' look, turns on his heel, and walks away. The moment he's out of the room, Ace calms down considerably and doesn't even lift his head when Mandy walks in. It just goes to show how much trust he has in her.

"I didn't mean to listen in, but I was coming to see you and heard the yelling from the hallway. Are you all right?" she says, coming to sit down on the couch, and pet Ace.

"Well, that's my dad, and that's as good as he gets. So feel free to turn around and run now if you were expecting some fine and caring in-laws," I grumble.

She reaches over and places her hand on my arm.

"Forget him. What do you want to do?"

"I need to figure it out."

I know that I have endless options here and I know that I could pursue anything. The counselors here have made that very clear, but none of it sounds appealing.

"So, it looks like today is the day that both of us get our asses chewed out," Mandy says, sinking into the couch, her body drooping.

"Why what happened?" I'm suddenly on guard.

"Rebecca showed up and cornered me in my office."

"Oh shit, are you serious? What did she want?"

The last thing I need is for Rebecca to have come here and started more trouble. Mandy and I just got back on solid ground, and things between us are really good.

"She started off by apologizing, so I thought things were going well, but she quickly changed direction. Then she started going on and on about how she isn't as okay with us as she thought she was and how if I had been a true friend I wouldn't have put her in this position."

My heart sinks, knowing I could never get between her and her best friend, especially when she has so few people in her life she can actually count on. But I want to be one of those people. I want to be in her life. I want to be the one who she comes to, to fix things.

Snapping my fingers at Ace to get him to move onto the floor, he follows directions and sits next to my feet. Then I reach over to Mandy and circle her waist, pulling her onto my lap. She lets out a little squeal of surprise and wraps her arm around my shoulders.

If she's going to end things between us, she's going to do it at least while she's in my arms, so I have one last memory of getting to hold her. One last memory where she's mine.

"What did you tell her?"

"I told her that she should have figured it out when I went to her, to begin with before things progressed between you and me. She then said that I should never have put her in this situation, to begin with, because now she's in a hard spot with her husband. And I said yeah, you're married, so you really don't have a say in this at all. That's when Noah asked her to leave."

"I'm happy to know he had your back."

"Both Noah and Lexi were there, and I'm glad. Their presence reminded me that I've come a long way from the girl I was back in high school."

"So, what do you want to do?"

"Do about what?" she asks.

"About us. The last thing I want is to slow down again or break up at all. But I'm not going to get between you and Rebecca either."

This makes her laugh out loud, full-on belly laughing, and judging by Ace's tilted up head, he's just as confused by it as I am.

"That's the last thing I want. I'm done letting other people control how I feel, what I do, comment on what I wear, or how I feel about myself. Rebecca has always been a good friend, but I placed way too much value on her opinion of me. I've grown a lot, especially since I've been working here, and I don't want to slow down or stop us either."

I don't want to lose Rebecca's friendship; she will bend over backward for you, but I wonder if the pregnancy hormones are causing her emotions, or if she really isn't okay with this.

"Good," I say, just before claiming her lips.

My dad being here is never a good sign, yet I can live in this moment right now, in this bubble where nothing else matters.

# Chapter 26

## Levi

After the disastrous meeting with my father, I wasn't at all surprised when his secretary called. My dad wanted to have lunch with me in a public location, of course, and not at Oakside. He would send a car for me and everything. It wasn't like I had much of a choice, but at least I would get a good meal out of it.

When my mother called me, I was surprised. Apparently, both she and my brother are in town with my dad, and they would like to have dinner with me without him. I guess my dad has some meeting, so he won't be there.

I agreed to both because I'm interested in what my dad has to say, and because I'd really like to see my mom and brother. Even though I know nothing good can come out of the lunch with my dad, I'm more nervous about my mom and brother because they are coming here to Oakside.

I'm sitting outside with Ace, and he's running around in the front yard as we wait for the car my father said he would send. My dad wasn't too happy when I made the condition that wherever we ate had to be someplace that was pet friendly because Ace was coming with me.

Ace does have his service dog training and a vest, but he hasn't been assigned to me as a service dog, and I didn't feel right using it to get into just any place.

Besides, making my dad have to work and rearrange his plans gives me a small feeling of joy. But in the end, he agreed.

A limousine pulls into the long driveway of Oakside as Noah steps up beside me.

"Your dad doesn't do anything small, does he?" Noah asks.

"Nope, he likes to flex his power anytime he gets a chance, especially when it comes to me, with how much I've apparently disappointed him."

"Well, I'll have my phone on me. You can send me an SOS text anytime you need, and I'll gladly come to your rescue."

I'm about to open my mouth and tell him I don't have a phone, but he's already pulling one out of his pocket and handing it to me.

"This one is yours. It has my number, Lexi's number, and Mandy's number already programmed in, along with Easton's number. You know all of us would be more than happy to come and rescue you if the lunch goes bad," he says, patting me on the shoulder before going back into the building.

Once the limo is at Oakside's entrance, I call Ace over, put his leash and harness on, which he hates. It's only about a fifteen-minute drive to the place that my dad picked out, and it's easy to see why. There's an entire outdoor dining area, which already has a few people dining with their dogs at the table.

Neither of us says a word until we are seated, and the waitress takes our drink orders.

"So, let's cut the shit and get right to the point, so we can enjoy our meal and then go our separate ways," I say and my dad actually chuckles.

"I see you've grown a stiffer backbone since your time in the service. That's good because you'll need it in business."

"There is no scenario where I would work in your business world. Or with anyone in your world, so it's not really worth wasting your time."

"You're right. This lunch is a waste of my time, but I'm doing it for your mother's sake. So at the very least, I can get her off my back about trying to help you. She wants you to come home, and so does your brother. You know we can find things for you to do. Maybe work with some charities."

I shouldn't be surprised that my father thinks so little of me, because he always has. But I guess he sees my injury as a weakness. It's interesting though because in a way it's a good thing as it's in direct contrast to what everyone at Oakside believes. Everyone there sees my missing leg as a strength that makes me a stronger person because of everything I've has overcome.

"If I want to work in the business world, I already have two offers on the table from two successful businessmen that are more successful than you. They have a higher net worth than you, and they are right here in this area of the country. The bonus is I wouldn't be working anywhere near you, and I'd be in direct competition with you."

I try not to smirk when he shifts in his chair, clearly uncomfortable with the thought of me being in direct competition with him. He may not see me with any worth, but I do know quite a bit about his business, enough to make me working for a competitor pretty lucrative. Not that I would ever sell him out like that, but I'm sure he thinks I would.

Our drinks arrive, and the waitress takes our food orders before he speaks again.

"Is that what you want to do? Sell out your own family and work with a company that only wants you for the information that you have?"

"Actually, neither of them knows who I am or about you. They offered me a job because of the skills I learned in the military, and they are valuable in the civilian world. But you didn't take the time to actually look into that, did you? I have a lot of doors open to me even if you don't think I do. If I don't want to take either of those jobs, the military will pay for me to go back to school and give me a place to live. Really, I can do anything I want to do and I don't need you again, so why are you here?"

"Well, you are family... "

"Don't even try to start with this 'I'm family, so of course I'm here' crap. You didn't care that I was family when I joined the military. In fact, you cared so little that you disowned me because I wanted to serve my country."

"Well, don't act like you joined to serve your country. It was to get away from me and we both know it. I want to make it clear that you are not to come home begging for money or for a place to stay. I offered all of that to you just now and you've turned me down, so that is going to be off the table. When you fall flat on your face, which we both know you will, don't come crying home to us."

"I could be homeless and living on the street and I still wouldn't come crying home to you. Besides, it would be more lucrative just to sell you out."

My father wants to go off on me, but he's holding himself back. As the waitress brings our food, his face is turning an alarming shade of bright red.

"Could you put mine in a box? I'm going to be heading out. This meeting is over."

She hurries off to put everything into a to-go container while I stand, and don't even say goodbye. When I get to the front door, the waitress is already there. She hands me the box and I get back into the car that my father sent and go back to Oakside, leaving him with the bill, which isn't much.

Back at Oakside, I share my lunch with Ace and start to wonder what the hell my mom and my brother could want to say. With any luck, dinner will go a lot better than the lunch just did.

· · · ● · · ● · · ·

I'm waiting in the lobby with Ace for my mom and my brother to get here. But it's Ace who spots them first and even though he's never met them, it's like he knows that they're related to me. He stands at attention and tilts his head slightly to the side so that his good eye has the best view of them.

The moment my mom spots me, she's in tears as she runs to me, giving me a huge hug.

"Oh, my baby. I was so terrified that you would get injured over there and the day we got that phone call was absolutely horrible. But look at you now! You would never know that you were seriously injured. It just shows how much hard work you've put into it and I'm so proud of you." My mom sobs on my shoulder.

It's such a night and day difference from my father. While I know my mother doesn't always agree with my father, she won't ever go against him, either. Though that makes me wonder why the secret dinner meeting tonight.

When she pulls away, my brother is right there and even he pulls me in for a hug.

"I'm so glad that you're okay and look like you're doing really well," he says in a very stoic tone, mirroring my dad, just a much nicer version.

"Oh, who is this guy?" My mom sits down on the chair next to her and starts petting Ace, who eats up her attention.

"Oh, your poor puppy! Look at your eye. You have been through so much, just like my baby boy, haven't you?" She starts rubbing behind his ears, which are his sweet spot.

"This is Ace. He was a military dog and was actually assigned to a guy that was in my unit. He and I were pretty good friends and Ace and I were good friends, too. After the explosion where I was injured, I guess there was another attack, and my buddy didn't make it. Ace here lost his eye and got some pretty nasty burns trying to save him."

"Oh, the poor boy. He's such a good dog. If you didn't see for yourself that he's missing an eye, you would never know, he's adapted so well," Mom says.

"Lexi, one of the owners of this place found him. Though she had no idea that I knew who he was, she was just going to bring him here and make him part of the Oakside family. But since the moment that we saw each other, he hasn't left my side."

"Well, I couldn't have timed this better myself." Lexi walks up and hands me a piece of paper. "Hi, I'm Lexi. My husband Noah and I run this place."

"Oh, thank you for taking care of my baby boy. I'm Levi's mom and this is his brother, Pike." My mom leans in and hugs Lexi, whose eyes go wide.

I look at her and mouth the word later, letting her know I'll explain everything. She nods and hugs my mom back as I look at the paper she handed me.

"What's this?" I ask.

"Well, Mandy, Paisley, and I have been working behind the scenes, and that's the paperwork that officially makes Ace your service dog. He's been trained, but I know you had issues because he hadn't been assigned to you, so now he's been officially assigned to you and is able to go anywhere you do in official service dog capacity."

"Are you serious?" I stand there in shock.

"Very serious. Paisley would like to work with him to do a little training especially to assist and help you. If there was ever a fall or issues with your prosthetic, Ace could help. If that will work for you?"

"What do you say, boy? You ready for a little training along with me?" Ace barks, as if he understands what she's saying.

"That's a yes for both of us. Thank you so much for this. You don't even understand what this means to me."

Lexi just shrugs like it's no big deal, even though it is a very big deal. "Just make sure you put in the work that Paisley asks you to do, that's all I ask. Now go enjoy your dinner." She leaves as my mom and my brother turn back to me.

They follow me into the dining room where we get our food and sit at a table in the corner out of the way.

"I'm going, to be honest. I hope this dinner goes a hell of a lot better than my lunch with Dad did earlier."

"Oh, Dad was pissed. But if I'm honest, I think he was a little proud of you too for standing up to him," Pike says.

"I'm not going to lie. I have thought about his offer. Only because it means I would get the two of you back in my life. I love and miss you both, but I don't know if giving up the rest of my life is something that I can do." I say as honestly as I can.

"We don't want that," Mom says.

"Listen, Mom and I have talked quite a bit, and we want you to be happy. I don't know what your next step is, and I don't know what you need to make it happen, but no matter what it is, it better not include taking Dad's offer," Pike says.

"What?" I ask, thinking there has to be an ulterior motive here.

"That came out a little wrong, but in short, Dad is no longer running the company. I've taken it over and he really has no power anymore. Though I can force him out and would do it in a heartbeat if it meant making sure that you're happy. We are both proud of you and if you want to be there, to run the family business because that's what you want, then you are more than welcome," Pike says.

"But we know that's never been your dream," Mom says. "Whatever your next step is, we want you to know that we support you. Just because your dad doesn't support you, doesn't mean that we won't be here for anything that you need."

"But you've never gone against what Dad has said, ever," I say in shock.

"What I'm about to say may sound horrible, but I'm going to say it anyway. Your dad has always held the purse strings. With your brother now running the company and your father not having that to hold over either of your heads, there really is no reason for me to stay with him anymore."

I drop my fork in complete shock.

"I've made sure that Mom has some stock in the company, and that she has enough to live on and a place to live wherever she wants to be. Mom spent her whole life raising us and running charities. I promised her that I would make sure that she's taken care of after she leaves Dad," Pike says.

So much has changed and the family that I remembered is no more. I spent so much time thinking my mom and my brother didn't see my dad like I did, didn't understand everything that he put me through. But I'm beginning to realize they did, however, they just dealt with it differently.

"Then I guess I should be honest and say I made a few veiled threats to Dad earlier today at lunch about not needing him and it was more lucrative to sell him out and sell the company out than it was to take up his offer. I would never do that even if he was still in charge, but I want you to know that it's not who I am."

"Oh, we know, and I actually had to bite my tongue to keep from laughing when Dad was going off about it earlier," Pike says.

Then we launch into a conversation, going over everything that we've missed the last several years from people to places and things that I've done in the service. Mom and Pike want to know everything and I tell them what I can, even everything about Mandy.

I leave out the issues with Mandy and Rebecca right now, and I definitely don't tell them that in the back of my mind I'm preparing for Mandy to choose Rebecca over me.

# Chapter 27

Before I even go into my office today, I want to check in on Levi. He had lunch with his dad yesterday and then dinner with his mom and brother, and I haven't had a chance to talk to him.

Lexi did say she kept an eye on them at dinner and that everything seemed to go well. There was no yelling or screaming and there were a lot of smiles.

He had a PT session first thing today, but he should be back in his room now. But I don't understand this pit in my stomach about going and visiting him today. Something just seems off.

When I get to this room, he's standing in front of the window, and I know that he does this when he needs to think about something. I lightly tap on the door, and he only turns his head slightly acknowledging that I'm there.

"I wanted to come and see how you were doing after your visits with your family yesterday," I say, but he doesn't answer me, and Ace is really agitated at his side.

He squeezes his hands into fists and it's like a live wire goes off. I don't think I've ever seen anything quite like it.

"I'm so sick and tired of people wanting an answer on what I plan to do with my life. I have no clue and I wish everyone would just leave me alone," he yells so loud that I can feel it in my bones.

Ace, who is a trained military dog, even tries to get away from him and hide behind the coffee table. After standing there in shock for only a minute, I turn and leave, not even realizing where I'm going until I'm standing in front of Lexi's house. Until she opens the front door and wraps me in a hug, I don't even realize I'm crying.

Instead of asking me what happened, she just takes me back to the sunroom, where we both sink into the couch and she simply holds me. Still not saying anything, she lets me cry until I'm ready to talk. Then I tell her what Levi said.

"You know," Lexi says, "everything seemed to be going very well and smoothly with him.

The visit with his mom and brother looked like a happy reunion. But I didn't see them leave, so I can't say things ended on a good note. He did have PT this morning, but that usually doesn't leave him in a mood like this. I'm sorry I can't give you any answers."

"I just don't know what to do."

"Well, I'm going to call an emergency girls' night tonight. You and I are going to hang out all day and we'll watch all those movies that we keep saying we're going to see but never have had time to. I'll send Noah to go get us incredibly unhealthy food and will blame it on baby cravings."

"That sounds perfect."

Before Noah shows up with our lunch, we're engrossed in the movies, and he doesn't even look surprised to see me there. So I'm guessing somewhere along the line Lexi texted him what was going on. He doesn't say a word about the food or about us being camped in the living room watching TV. He just drops the food off, gives his wife a kiss, and goes back out the door.

"I hope you know how incredibly lucky you are. What you and Noah have is extremely rare," I say, digging into my fries.

"I do know. But I think that you'll have that too before you know it."

We watch a few more movies before the girls show up. All of them have brought food for dinner and with Lexi being the only pregnant one, they brought bubbly apple cider for her and alcohol for the rest of us.

Once we're all sitting in the sunroom with the food spread out on the coffee table and drinks in our hands, I look at everyone and groan.

"What was that for?" Paisley, who's sitting next to me asks.

"I just realized I'm the only not married one here."

Paisley looks around and then giggles because it's true. Besides her and Lexi, also here are Brooke and Kaitlyn, who are nurses at Oakside. Both of them fell in love over Christmas and have been all happy and googly eyed just like Lexi and Paisley.

"We need more single girls in our group," I grumble.

"Well, Noah's oldest sister will be joining us next year. But if I'm honest, there's probably going to be some girls' nights without her because talking about my husband to her would be just weird." Lexi says and everyone giggles again.

"Okay ladies, night rules," Lexi says and holds up one finger. "One, no drinking and driving. There are guest bedrooms upstairs and downstairs and couches around the house. Crash anywhere you want and you are always welcome to stay."

She holds up a second finger. "Two, we are friends first. We are not bosses and employees, we are friends, and we are here as friends. Venting about work is okay. Venting about patients is okay and venting about guys is encouraged. We are here to support each other."

Then she holds up a third finger. "Three. What is talked about at ladies' night stays at ladies' night. This is a safe place and we're free to express our feelings. What is talked about in this room doesn't leave this room. Got it?"

Everyone nods and agrees. Though we've heard this speech so many times, we can practically recite it word for word.

"Good. Now we are here for Mandy," Lexi says and then all eyes shoot to me.

"Well, if I'm going to spill my guts, somebody needs to refill my drink." I hold up my cup, and Brooke fills it up with more sangria. After taking a big sip, I then start at the beginning.

I tell them about how I knew Levi from before and how he dated Rebecca in high school. When Levi and I saw each other here, it was simply a friendship. But then, slowly but surely, not even realizing what was happening, it became more. I tell them how I chickened out about telling Rebecca at first and her reaction when I finally told her.

Then I tell them about the disastrous lunch and my meeting with Rebecca afterward. Finally, I relate how Levi's father showed and his time with him yesterday all the way up to him blowing up at me this morning. When I'm done, I set down my empty glass, that was filled up twice more as I let everything out.

"Well, I'll go first since my situation with Easton is probably the closest to yours. He was my brother's best friend growing up and to say that I was shocked when I saw him here was an understatement. I'd always had a crush on him, but when I saw him again, I wanted to help reach him because he was just so shut off from the world." Taking a sip of her sangria, she stops to think.

Her dog, Molly, sensing that Paisley's memories are too painful and distressing, climbs up onto the sofa between her and me and rests her head on Paisley's shoulder. Molly is a service dog who helps the men at Oakside. Even though she's not Paisley's service dog, she is her dog.

"There was a point where Easton was doing really well, and our relationship was doing great, and then it was like reality crushed in on him. It was in the form of my brother, but it sounds like Levi's reality crashed in on him with his family. You know the guys exist in this bubble at Oakside and it's so easy for them to forget about anything outside in the real world."

"I've seen it happen so many times with my patients," Kaitlyn says. "When they're so close to having the big breakthrough, they shut down. They close off because it scares them and they're truly terrified because it means they're so exposed emotionally."

Kaitlyn is a nurse at Oakside, and she is Levi's daytime nurse. She was also Easton's nurse.

"I can back that up. It was the same way at the hospital with all the men," Brooke says. She's the head nurse at Oakside, and Lexi and Noah met her at the hospital when she was

Noah's nurse. Then when they started Oakside, they brought her over with them.

"Though I think Noah was the exception to the rule. I don't think he had a big setback like the rest of the guys here have," Brooke says.

"But we all know Lexi and Noah are the exception to the rule. From the very beginning, their relationship was completely different, especially how Lexi met Noah in the hospital," Kaitlyn says and everyone agrees.

"The best thing you can do is just let him know that you're there, but give him his space. This is something he has to do on his own. And it's going to take the time it took Easton, at least a month. I think it took Teddy longer than that to find his way back to Mia. So just be patient. While I know it's not easy, it'll be worth it," Paisley says.

The night continues as everyone gives an update on what they've been up to the past month or so since our last girls' night. Brooke has been slowly winning over her husband Luke's sister, Gabbie, who was none too happy about the two of them getting together.

Kaitlyn's dad just found his own place not too far from her and her husband, Grayson. When her father moved down here from Kentucky, he moved in with them until he got settled. You can tell Kaitlyn is so happy to have him close.

"Well, Easton brought up the big C word recently, and I have no idea where I stand on the issue," Paisley says.

We all look at each other, a bit confused before I ask.

"What's the big C word?"

"Children. With Lexi being pregnant, he wants to start having kids. Don't get me wrong, I want kids, and I especially want kids with Easton, but I think I would rather it just happened as it did for Lexi and Noah. Rather than trying to get pregnant, because planning it makes me too nervous."

"So, tell him that. And for the record, I'm still nervous as hell. But yeah, you're right. When it just happens, then it's time to just strap on your big girl pants and head straight on into the fire because there's no backing out. I couldn't have imagined planning this, or I'd have been a nervous wreck." Lexi says.

As the night goes on, all of us that can drink have a few more. Then the guys show up to pick up their girls. Apparently, they had a guys' night over at Oakside, where they played some cards out on the back porch.

Noah and Easton are good friends, but it's great to see Luke and Grayson making friends with them as well.

"Looks like I'm the only one camping out here this time," I say.

"Well, that just means you have your pick of guest bedrooms," Lexi says.

"Actually, I think I'm going to crash on the sofa out here. Something about the sunroom is calming, plus it's supposed to be a really pleasant night tonight."

Lexi gives me a hug and before heading to bed, she says, "Everything will look different tomorrow you'll see."

# Chapter 28

It's been two weeks since I snapped at Mandy. Two weeks since I've been able to talk to her, to hold her, or even just have lunch with her, and there is this dark spot in my life where she used to be.

After my dad's visit, I started talking with my therapist more freely. I guess there was a lot there to go over, and not just from my military time, but from my childhood as well.

My brother made good on his promise and assisted my mother with finding her own place. When my mother filed for divorce, it turned my father's world upside down. I'm actually very happy to be on the other side of the country and not in that mess. Yet I do worry for my brother and mom, and that has been part of my therapy sessions.

I finally opened up about the blast where I lost my leg. While that was something I never wanted to relive, I knew it was something I had to at least talk to him about. Every night since, I've been having nightmares again, unless I take medication. But I know that once I work this out, they'll go away just like they did before.

Trying to figure out what I want to do once I leave Oakside has been hard, and I've not gotten any answers. My counselor is getting a little frustrated, and that's what I've been talking to my therapist about today.

"Levi. Did you hear a word of what I just said to you?" Dr. Tate, my therapist, asks.

"No, I'm sorry. My mind is anywhere but here today."

"And what were you thinking about just now?"

I hesitate for only a minute. Normally I would just brush him off, but I've been forcing myself to open up to him, even when it's extremely uncomfortable.

"Honestly, I was thinking about how long it's been since I've had any time with Mandy."

"I have a theory about why you're having such a problem deciding your next moves."

"Well, by all means, don't hold back. Not that you haven't before," I'm truly interested in what he has to say.

"I think you can't make up your mind because all the options that have been laid in front of you will lead you away from Mandy."

I open my mouth to tell him that's crazy, but is it? Taking the job with Teddy or Owen would mean moving to another state. Going to work for my brother would be moving across the country. Several of the other schooling options that were brought up to me were all out of state, with jobs that wouldn't be in Georgia when I was finished.

It's something I think about and chew on for the rest of the day. But I can't get the thought out of my head. If two weeks without her makes me feel like this, how would I feel after months without her? Being away from her in another state?

Tonight I have another nightmare. When I finally wake up from it, I turn on every light in my room, even though there are not enough lights to push away the dark shadows. When there's a light knock at the door, I about jump out of my skin.

"I didn't mean to scare you. I was here checking on another patient and saw your lights turn on and wanted to make sure you were okay," Noah says.

"I'm not saying this to be mean, but seriously, do I look okay?" I say in what I try to make a joking tone.

But Noah sees right through it. Walking into my room and closing the door behind him, he sits down in the chair next to me. "Want to talk about it?" he asks.

My gut instinct is to say no, and I'll work it out. Or I could tell him that it's not really any of his business, but instead, I take a minute and think. After taking some deep breaths, I come to the conclusion that maybe I do need someone else's opinion on this.

"My therapist thinks that the reason I can't decide what I want to do is that all the options lead me away from Mandy," I tell him and then watch his reaction.

"Well, it makes sense. I guess the question you need to ask yourself is if she is someone who you want in your life. After all, you are making all these important decisions and need to know. If she's not the one, then you just need to bite the bullet and pick something. If you see a future with her, then it's time to come up with a different plan."

I think about how I felt over the past few weeks without her here. I don't like the space between us, and if I'm being honest with myself, what I feel for her is a hell of a lot stronger than anything I felt for any of my ex-girlfriends. Not that there were many.

Since all this started with us, something has shifted in the last few months. When I look into my future, I know without a shadow of a doubt, I see her there.

"She's my Lexi," is all I have to say.

Noah stands and walks slowly through the door before he turns around.

"You could always go back to school, get a degree, and work here at Oakside and be with Mandy. The school down in Savannah is excellent, and I know because my sister is starting there next semester. You just have to figure out what you want to do." At his words, suddenly a whole new world of possibilities has opened up in front of me.

He leaves, closing the door behind him and my nighttime nurse peeks her head in to make sure I'm okay. I assure her I am, and start turning off the lights and getting back into bed where Ace joins me.

I'd be crazy not to admit that Ace has been a huge part of my recovery, and while I know not every guy here gets a dog assigned to him, I don't know where I'd be without him.

Now I guess the biggest question I have is what's going on with Rebecca and Mandy. I never want to get in between them, but if Rebecca isn't all right with us dating, I'm not sure how Mandy's going to handle it.

Guess the only thing I can do is talk to her, and pray that I'm not too late.

# Chapter 29

I'm in my office, lost in spreadsheets and numbers, when Levi appears at my office door. I feel him even before I see him, and I had no idea that was even possible.

"I was hoping we could talk," he says.

Since I've been working all morning, I could use a break.

"Yeah, come in." I say as I save what I was working on.

"Let's go for a walk. You look like you could use it." I stand and follow him upstairs to the front porch.

We start toward the garden, neither of us saying anything. I figure if he wants to talk, he has something to say, and I will let him say it. Ace walks right by Levi's side, but I can tell he's itching to run.

"I've decided what I want to do when I get out of here." He says, shoving his hands into his pockets.

My heart sinks. He's doing so much better and now that he's made a decision, he will be released soon. Then he'll be off on whatever new journey he has decided, and that means away from me.

"I want to go to school to help train service dogs like Paisley does, and then come back and work here at Oakside. Paisley and Easton are looking to start a family and she doesn't want to work when she does, she just wants to do the volunteer stuff," he says.

It takes a minute to realize his entire plan revolves around coming and working here.

"Levi, that's great news. You'll be able to help the patients so much since you have been in their shoes."

"That's what I was thinking, too. There are classes in Savannah and the military covers school and housing for me, so I can stay in the area." He says as we enter the garden.

The walls give this place a European feel. Lexi said when they were building it, she wanted it to be an escape for the patients, and she didn't want them to see the outside world and they can't. They can feel like they are anywhere but here.

There are plenty of places to sit and relax, along with several fountains and a small waterfall. The water sounds alone are calming. This place is already pretty large, so there could be several people here and you wouldn't be in each other's space. Though, it looks like we have the place to ourselves now.

"I'm sorry for snapping at you the way I did. It wasn't about you, but a combination of everything from my dad, and then PT and my other appointments. Whoever walked through the door, I would have snapped at, unfortunately, it was you."

Mandy gives me an understanding smile, saying, "I get that being here isn't easy and I don't expect things to be all sunshine and roses. Paisley says Easton was that way when he had his breakthrough, so I was hoping that was what was happening with you."

He finally wraps his arm around my waist and pulls me to his side.

"I like to think it was. Though I hate that I took it out on you, and I hate the space that's been between us ever since. But I won't lie, it was what I needed."

Once we get towards the back of the garden by the waterfall, there's a picnic set up.

"Is this for us?" I ask.

"It's for you. I was hoping I could get you to join me for lunch."

Something about this moment just seems bigger. It's as if I know that if I sit down and have lunch with him and we move on from this fight, I'm choosing him over Rebecca. I hate fighting with Rebecca, but I don't think I can walk away from Levi right now either. In fact, I know I can't. So I smile, and sit down on the blankets that are set out on the ground.

With a little maneuvering, he joins me, and the first thing he pulls out is a bone that he gives to Ace, who happily takes it and starts working the bone over.

"I guess I had a bit of a breakthrough during our break as well," I say as he starts pulling out food.

"Oh yeah, and what would that be?"

"That Rebecca not being okay with us is her problem. As much as I would hate to lose her as a friend, she has her own life and her own family to worry about now. Sometimes people are in your life for only certain parts of it and they're not meant to be there forever."

"I really hate the thought of me being what drives you and her apart, but I can honestly say I agree. Sometimes people are in your life for only a certain amount of time."

He sets his food down and looks over at me.

"I love you, Mandy," his eyes bore into mine.

"I love you, too," I say, barely above a whisper before leaning in and pulling his lips to mine.

It's been so long since I've been in his arms that when he wraps them around me, I melt into him. This feels right and where I am meant to be.

The kiss is way too short, and I could spend the rest of the day kissing him, but I'm excited to eat the lunch he planned for us, too.

As we eat, we talk and catch up on what had been happening over the last few weeks. I was excited to tell him about the donation, and the plans that we've been putting into action. He was impressed that we've gotten everything ready to start construction on what will be the third floor.

Going on, I tell him we decided to spend a little more and bring in extra guys to try to get it done faster during the day so as not to disturb the patients for long. Because it will be noisy until we get it finished, but with Lexi's dad heading the crew, we know he can get it done.

Then he tells me about finally opening up to his therapist, and how that helped him pick what he wants to do. Noah has been a big supporter of him working here at Oakside as well, and that doesn't surprise me. Noah likes to try to keep everybody close, and bonds with everyone.

While I'm having a great time, I'm feeling like Levi is nervous. Maybe there's something that he needs to tell me, but he's scared to, and I don't want to bring it up because we're having fun.

When Ace finishes his bone, he gets up and starts running around the garden, sniffing at different flowers and chasing a butterfly here and there. When he finally tires himself out, he comes back to us, collapses on the edge of the blanket, and falls asleep almost instantly.

"Well, I guess I can't stall any longer. I had a bigger reason for bringing you out here. As you know, I've had a lot of decisions to make over the last few weeks, and I was talking with my therapist because there was this block that I couldn't seem to get past and make any decisions. Then he said something that shocked the hell out of me."

I'm almost scared to ask what it is, but thankfully he continues his story without me saying a word.

"He said that I couldn't make a decision because every decision was leading me away from you. And he was right. Once I had a choice that kept me here, I felt at peace with it, and I knew that was the path that I was going to take."

My heart races as he reaches into his pocket and pulls out a small box. I can't breathe at all. He maneuvers so he is on one knee, a move I know he practiced which makes it all the more perfect.

"I did a lot of thinking and I realized that you are my future, even with the rest of it uncertain. But I am certain about you. Will you do me the great honor of being my wife?" He opens the box to the most stunning engagement ring I think I have ever seen. It's more gorgeous than anything I've ever owned in my life.

"Levi..." I gasp, not able to get any other words out.

Looking at me with so much hope on his face, I know now that I have never been more certain of anything in my entire life. But there is one more thing that I have to know.

"We never discussed this, but I need to know before I give you my answer. Do you want kids?" I ask, with tears streaming down my face.

A huge smile takes over his face.

"I want as many kids as you want to give me. But I want to be a better father than my father was, and I want to help them do whatever they want to do. I want to give you the family that you never had, that will love you unconditionally no matter what. While I can't promise you an amazing father-in-law, I can tell you right now my mom is beyond excited to meet you, and my brother is already making plans to spoil future nieces and nephews."

"Yes, I will absolutely marry you!"

His hands shake as he removes the ring from the box and places it on my finger. When I see how big the rock actually is on my hand, I gasp. We take a few of the traditional 'I said yes' photos, and I assume he sends them to his mom and brother as he sits down beside me.

"My dad built his company from the ground up, and he wasn't always the asshole we all know and hate today. When I was born, my dad gave this ring to my mom as a gift. At our dinner, when I told my mom that I was certain that you were it for me, she took it off her finger and said that this ring was a symbol of me coming into the world, and it should be a symbol of our new life together."

I don't even realize tears are freely streaming down my face until he reaches up and wipes them away with his thumb.

"I can't wait to meet your mom and brother," I say, admiring my ring.

"Good, because they can't wait to meet you, either. So much so that when they knew I was going to propose today, they decided they had to be here," he says just as a woman and man walk into the garden.

As they walk toward us, both have smiles on their faces.

"This is my mom and my younger brother, Pike. And guys, this is Mandy, and as you can tell by the gigantic smile on both of our faces, she said yes."

Levi's mom is a lot younger than I thought she'd be, and she has Levi's eyes. Startling me, she lunges forward and pulls me into a welcoming hug.

"Levi told me that you don't have a family, and while our family is far from perfect, I am beyond excited to have you be part of it. I always wanted a daughter, and I didn't get one, so I would be honored if one day you decide to call me Mom."

By the time she pulls away, I'm in tears, and there are tears in her eyes threatening to fall as well.

"Well, I can't say I ever wanted a sister while I was growing up, but it will be nice to have some nieces and nephews to spoil. I plan to be the cool uncle. The one who buys them all the loud and messy toys, and then sends them home to Mom and Dad," Pike says, smirking.

He may be Levi's younger brother, but the two of them look to be almost the same age. Maybe it's the suit Pike is wearing. He wears his hair just a little bit longer than Levi, and it has a slight curl at the end.

Pike gives me a side hug, but when he turns to Levi, he pulls him in for a big hug and he has a smile on his face to match.

Packing up the picnic, we head back up to the main building as we talk and start making future plans. His mom wants to be as involved in the wedding planning as much as I want her to be. Just the fact that she's willing to step back if I don't want her involved means a lot to me. But to be completely honest, it would be a great relief not to have to do it alone.

When they find out Levi's plans of staying here and working at Oakside, his brother starts talking about buying a house out here so that they can come and visit more often. Also, so that his mom can choose to stay anytime that she wants.

That night, as his mom and his brother get ready to go to their hotel room, his brother says something that I think shocks everyone.

"You know dad started the business here and had headquarters in Atlanta for such a long time. He's explained the move to Denver several times, but I think it might have everything to do with what was going on at the time. But it might be time to move the headquarters back or consider opening a second office in Savannah. I think both Mom and I would be happier being back here full-time."

"That would be perfect. But let's not open that can of worms until after the divorce is final," Levi's mom says.

"I agree. I'd love to have you back here all the time," Levi says, and I agree.

And just like that, I have the family that I always dreamed about, but with a few minor adjustments.

• • • • • • • • • •

It's been a week since Levi and I got engaged. The day we got engaged, he had called Kade and told him. Then yesterday he let me read Kade's latest letter.

For our honeymoon, Kade invited us to come stay in one of his luxury villas! He said he would cover all the costs, even transportation out there. Also, his family wants to meet us. I hadn't realized how close they had gotten. But Levi says they talk and text all the time and still send care packages with their letters.

Today I'm having lunch with Rebecca. Since the day she stormed out of my office, we haven't spoken, but I want her to hear this from me and not from someone else.

If I'm being honest, I also want to know if she's going to be in our lives or not. Because Levi and I are starting a whole new chapter, I need to know who is going to be in it.

Rebecca and I are meeting at a restaurant in Savannah since Dale is here for another meeting. Before I'm ready to say what I came here for, I do my best to keep my left hand hidden because I don't want the ring to give away anything.

No sooner do we place our orders with the waitress, than she turns to me.

"I can tell that you have something to say, and I think we should start with you just getting it out and go from there."

"You're right. I came here so that you would hear this from me and not from anyone else. But Levi asked me to marry him, and I said yes," I say, setting both my hands on the table in front of me, no longer hiding the ring.

Her eyes go wide, and she doesn't say anything at first, but her eyes make their way down to the ring on my hand, which is easily double the size of hers. When she got engaged, I swore her ring was the biggest thing I had ever seen, so that's saying something.

"I didn't realize you guys were that serious," she says softly.

"You never really asked, and I never got a chance to tell you. At the lunch was when that should have been discussed, but you wanted to take a trip down memory lane instead. And then, after the fight in my office, I decided I wasn't going to let you stop us because by then, we were already in too deep."

Looking out the window next to us, she remains silent. Though she looks sad and normally, I would do anything I could to comfort her, but I can't fall down that path of choosing her over Levi. As Levi is going to be my husband, I have to choose him over all else now.

Soldiering on, I say, "I know how things were left the last time we talked, and they weren't good. Again, I just wanted you to hear this for me. I'm not expecting you to be happy about this or even want to be part of our wedding. Though I would hate that, I have to be all right with it. So, the ball is in your court. You can be as involved in our life as much as you want or as little as you want."

When she looks back at me, there are tears in her eyes and she gives me a wobbly smile.

"When we were planning my wedding, I kept thinking I can't wait 'til I get to do this with you because I knew that you getting married would mean so much more. You would be getting a family and I'm so happy that you're finally getting that, even if it's one as messed up as Levi's." She tries to laugh but fails.

"I truly am happy for both of you, and want to be involved, and I want to be friends. Though I can't promise it won't be weird hearing about the two of you. But I'm sure in a few years I will get over it and it will just be a funny story that you can tell people at parties and eventually tell our kids."

"Then I just have one question for you," I say fighting the tears that are threatening to fall.

"Always. You can ask me anything that hasn't changed."

"Will you be my maid of honor?"

"Yes!" she squeals, causing people to turn and see what is going on around us.

She jumps up and wraps me in a hug, and I can't help but laugh. I feel like how it used to be in high school where it was her and me against the world.

As we sit back down, she launches into wedding planning mode. And just like that, all is right in my world again.

# Epilogue

I love my job teaching those who've lost their sight how to get around in the world. Mainly, I work with soldiers at the military hospital, but when Lexi reached out for me to help someone at the Oakside rehabilitation home, I jumped at the chance.

Spending the last few weeks getting the room ready, I also took some time familiarizing myself with the place before my patient got there. I had his information but not his name, and maybe in hindsight, I should have pressed for the name. But there's no way I could have known.

When I walked into Oakside today, I was so thrilled, hoping that if things went well, I could start working with more patients here. My patient was brought in a few days ago, and has had a little bit of time to settle in before meeting me today.

But as I stand in the doorway and stare at the man I thought I would never see again, I'm frozen in place and can't speak or move.

"You know I can hear someone is there. It's not nice to just stare at the blind man, you know," he grumbles.

"Sorry. I think I have the wrong room." I squeak out, turn and run back to Lexi.

"I can't do this," I say the moment I meet her at the reception desk.

"What? Why not?" She says full of concern.

"Because Gavin is my ex, the one who shattered my heart," I admit as her eyes go wide.

I expect her to understand and agree and say that she will find someone else. What I don't expect is the smile that slowly takes over her face.

"That means that you're the perfect person for this job. You know him better than anyone else will. I'm not going to let you out of this that easy."

Groaning because internally I know she's right, even if I really dislike her right now. I take a deep breath and go back to Gavin's room.

On the way there, I somehow convince myself that if I act professionally there's no way he'll realize that it's me. This is crazy because he may have lost his sight, but he hasn't lost his hearing. Yet again, I convince myself that my voice is not the same as it was all those years ago.

We've both changed since he joined the military, so there's no way that he'll recognize me. If I keep things professional, I can help him until I can convince Lexi to find someone else to take over.

With my plan in place, I slip up to his door and knock.

"Who's there?"

"I'm your therapist, here to help you learn how to get around. I figured today we'll start and see how well you know your room, and I'll teach you how to navigate better." I say in my most professional voice.

His body tenses as he stands up, and he turns towards me. Still convinced that this will work, I don't expect the words that come out of his mouth.

"Lauren? You're the last person I expected to find here," he says with anger in his voice.

"Yeah, well, that makes two of us."

· · · · ● · ● · · ·

Want Lauren and Gavin's Story? **Grab Saving Gavin!**

Want to know more about Kade and Seaview? Start the duet with **<u>Sunrise</u>**!

You can also get Mason and Paige's in **Saving Mason**!

# Connect with Kaci Rose

Website
Facebook
Kaci Rose Reader's Facebook Group
TikTok
Instagram
Twitter
Goodreads
Book Bub
Join Kaci Rose's VIP List (Newsletter)

# More Books By Kaci Rose

See all of Kaci Rose's Books

**Oakside Military Heroes Series**
**Saving Noah –** Lexi and Noah
**Saving Easton –** Easton and Paisley
**Saving Teddy –** Teddy and Mia
**Saving Levi –** Levi and Mandy
**Saving Gavin –** Gavin and Lauren

**Mountain Men of Whiskey River**
**Take Me To The River –** Axel and Emelie
**Take Me To The Cabin –** Pheonix and Jenna
**Take Me To The Lake –** Cash and Hope
**Take Me To The Mountain –** Bennett and Willow
**Chasing the Sun Duet**
**Sunrise –** Kade and Lin
**Sunset –** Jasper and Brynn

## Standalone Books
**She's Still The One** – Dallas and Austin
**Stay With Me Now** – David and Ivy
**Texting Titan** - Denver and Avery
**Accidental Sugar Daddy** – Owen and Ellie

**Saving Mason** - Mason and Paige
**Midnight Rose**
**Committed Cowboy** – Whiskey Run Cowboys
**Billionaire's Marigold** - Dakota and Grant

# Please Leave a Review!

I love to hear from my readers! Please **head over to your favorite store and leave a review** of what you thought of this book!

Manufactured by Amazon.ca
Bolton, ON

33636397R00181